Bab el-Oued

Bab el-Oued

MERZAK ALLOUACHE

translated by
ANGELA M. BREWER

A THREE CONTINENTS BOOK
LYNNE RIENNER PUBLISHERS
BOULDER & LONDON

Published in the United States of America and elsewhere by
Lynne Rienner Publishers, Inc.
1800 30th Street, Boulder, Colorado 80301
www.rienner.com

First published in French by Editions du Seuil. © Editions du Seuil, April 1995

This is a work of fiction. Names, characters, places, and incidents are the
products of the author's imagination or are used fictitiously, and any resemblance
to actual persons (living or dead), events, or locales is entirely coincidental.

Library of Congress Cataloging-in-Publication Data
Allouache, Merzak.
  [Bab el-Oued. English]
  Bab el-Oued / by Merzak Allouache : translated by Angela M.
Brewer.
    p. cm.
  ISBN 978-0-89410-859-4 (hc : alk. paper)
  ISBN 978-0-89410-860-0 (pb : alk. paper)
    1. Algiers (Algeria)—Social life and customs—Fiction.
I. Title.
PQ3989.2.A3786B3313   1998
843—dc21   98-38470
                                                    CIP

Printed and bound in the United States of America

Translator's Foreword

Angela M. Brewer

Bab el-Oued began as a film, *Bab el-Oued City,* a humorous as well as serious work that enjoyed a certain success. The author, Merzak Allouache, wanted to develop more fully some of the themes and characters introduced in the film, so he decided to write the book. This explains the cinematic quality of the short chapters and sentences.

There are many Arabic words and French idioms in the original, French-language edition of the book, and I was tempted at first to cut out many of them, thinking that English speakers might find it hard to cope with the mixed-language sentences. But on talking with an Algerian friend, I realized that this would not be acceptable, that it would be a betrayal, since, as she said, "we speak like that all the time." Hence, I have provided the glossary below. I hope nonetheless that the story speaks for itself, and that English-speaking readers will enjoy the tale.

Glossary

Allah Akbar!   God is great!
arbatache   an agricultural region
banks   free of charge
bayane   official stamp
bouh'alik!   untranslatable directly, but akin to "you must be joking!"
boussaadi   a sharp mountain knife
bouzelouf   sheep's head
bromitch   a bait made of bread and other substances likely to attract fish

burnous a long garment with a hood

chaabi a kind of popular music

chahada a prayer, the credo

chechia a headdress made of a piece of cloth wound around the head

choukchouka a dish made of grilled peppers and garlic marinated in olive oil

d'hor afternoon, as in afternoon prayer

dlala (woman selling) black market goods; flea market

fartas bald

fitna violent clashes between dissenting groups within the same religious faith

FLN Front de Libération National, the Algerian nationalist movement fighting for independence

gandoura traditional, but not Islamist, costume for men

gouars foreigners, especially Europeans

goudroun strong black coffee

hadjib shutting away

half-half milky coffee

harissa a spicy sauce eaten with couscous

hidjab the Islamic headscarf for women

hogra injustice, contempt, being left out; a prevalent feeling among the young people, and a very important factor behind the violence in Algeria today

horma sacrosanct respect for women; a place from which men are excluded

jebel mountain village

jellaba the traditional long robe for women

jihad Holy War

keffiyeh headdress

maquis the name given to the guerrilla soldiers who took to the bush, literally, "thick formation of shrubs"

medh a popular kind of religious music

meïda round low table

minbar the pulpit in the mosque

mouhafada the headquarters of the FLN (Front de Libération National) in a town

nar t'achaal fantastic, fiery

OAS Organisation de l'Armée Secrète (the Secret Army), a group of French settlers who used terrorist tactics to try to prevent Algeria's independence

oudaâtes meal prepared as an offering

pied-noir the French settlers in Algeria; literally "black foot," from the black patent leather shoes they wore *qamis* (chemise) a long, white robe, tailored like a shirt, worn by the Islamists

rai a lively brand of pop music that spread from the Maghreb (North African) countries and became very popular elsewhere, for example, France

rass rass man to man

redjla macho

sadaq'a giving money to the poor, alms

Salaam a'leikoum peace be with you, the traditional greeting when people meet

s'hour meal taken during the fasting period of Ramadan, just before sunrise

smina fatso

strounga bomb

taghout infidel

tawil dough, cash

trabendo smuggling, the black market

wilaya region

Places Mentioned

Bain de Chevaux Horse Dip Beach

Climat de France Climate of France, a district high up in Algiers, also punningly known as Climate of Suffering (Climat de Souffrance)

Houbel monument the name given by the Islamists to a modern monument in a new, expensive, sophisticated shopping area

Kabylia a mountainous region of Algeria, south of the capital and home of the Berber people

Notre Dame d'Afrique the large Catholic basilica in Algiers; also the name of a neighborhood, near the hill of Sidi Bennour

Place des Trois Horloges Three Clocks Square

Rocher Carré Square Rock, by the sea, where the drug addicts hang out and where the fight takes place between Boualem and Saïd

Bab el-Oued

1

DESPITE BEING FIRMLY LASHED TO THE MOSQUE'S MINARET, THE three loudspeakers were so heavily buffeted by the wind that they seemed ready to drop off. They crackled slightly when Imam Rabah coughed. After clearing his throat he solemnly and sententiously pronounced the holy words to which there is no response, "In the name of Allah, the merciful, the compassionate."

The sermon could now begin.

"Cleanliness, brothers! How, in an Islamic country, where the Holy Koran teaches us cleanliness, can we bear the sights we have to face every day? Don't you see these heaps of filth strewn across our streets, piling up even in front of our doorways?"

The sky above the city of Algiers was unusually sultry and red this early afternoon. The climate had been suffocating ever since the night before. Out of nowhere, in the middle of the night, a strong southerly wind had whipped up, bringing with it countless clouds heavy with sand. After a few hours, the wind, as if obeying a mysterious command, suddenly died down. Throughout the whole morning the clouds remained stationary, hovering above the city, coating it with a heavy stagnant layer, creating an ominous atmosphere. Then the wind, carrying new clouds, had begun to blow up again.

Since then it had not stopped.

Boualem is asleep, his body flung across the bed. Perspiration glues his T-shirt to his skin. His constantly moving head shows he is deep in abnormally agitated sleep. The room is in semidarkness. The narrow window lets in only a wan ray of light; the pale blue paint on the walls is flaking in places because of the damp. A few small objects and some old-fashioned furniture clutter up the room; there is a slightly rickety bed, which is in fact only a bed base with a foam mattress on top.

The Imam's booming voice fills the room. "And we pass these heaps of filth each and every day without even noticing them, without bothering about them. Just as if we were blind. We don't see them, we don't smell them. They don't exist. Because we don't want to see them, to smell them, we don't want them to exist . . ."

AT THE OTHER END of the neighborhood, in the area around the Hayat mosque, one of the most famous in Bab-el-Oued, the narrow streets are thronged as usual by a tightly packed crowd impervious to the vagaries of the weather. In this crowd, the immaculate whiteness of the thousands of long white *qamis* proudly worn by the young believers with their well-grown beards predominates; they are sitting erect on long mats, interested not in the strange redness of the sky but in the strident, hypnotic, familiar voice of Imam Rabah, carefully choosing his words in colloquial Arabic so as to be understood by all.

"We blot them out. We don't want to know. We simply don't notice them. Yet in our discussions we talk of cleanliness and hygiene. We proudly claim to be 'Muslims, the cleanest of all human beings in this wicked world below.' And then, complacently, we fall asleep . . . No, my brothers! Talking is not enough; we must act! The scourge is growing every day . . . In the name of God, the merciful, the compassionate, we must open our eyes to the dirt creeping up on us and taking over our neighborhoods."

The crowd, approving and determined, yells "Allah Akbar!" The sound echoes through the district making the windowpanes rattle. The Imam's voice continues at the same raised pitch, amplified by the three loudspeakers, made in Germany and fixed to the top of the minaret. The message is relayed by a long length of gray cable running from the mosque to the loudspeaker set up on the terrace of a neighboring block of flats and which in turn is connected to another loudspeaker perched on the terrace of yet another block of flats a few doors away.

In this way a whole web of sound was spun from terrace to terrace by a long length of gray cable connecting one loudspeaker to another, encircling the neighborhood just as powerfully as the clouds above the city. A "sacred spider's web," as the militants, on the verge of tears, a sob in their voice, liked to call it, referring to the famous "spider's web of bygone times which protected the prophet Mohammed, may his name be praised, when he sought refuge in the cave."

As on every Friday, the streets near the mosque are clogged by a gigantic inextricable traffic jam that two policemen, suffocating in their too hot, unseasonable blue uniforms, are halfheartedly trying to disentangle.

The gray cable swaying in the wind leads to the terrace of a block of flats a few hundred meters away from the mosque as the crow flies. This building, right in the heart of Bab el-Oued, at 13

Ramdane-Kahlouche Street, imposing and six stories high, is typical of the colonial architecture of the turn of the century. Now, with the passing of the years, the lack of maintenance, the pollution, and various kinds of damage, it is just as ugly as most of the other large buildings in the city. Its shabby, old, flaking paintwork, devastated by the damp, its crumbling cornices and balconies (so dilapidated that from time to time a piece comes away and hits the passerby) make it look like a large monster nearing the end of its life.

In one of his first sermons, Imam Rabah had indeed remonstrated with the faithful. "Your buildings are so shabby they look as if someone is gobbling up a piece each day. Tell me brothers, tell me truthfully, do you really like the taste of concrete? Are you unaware that Islam is the religion of cleanliness?"

The faithful, of course, had yelled a resounding "Allah Akbar!" glancing furtively at one another, accusing the neighbors' children, those wild, tough, future good-for-nothings, of being the miserable creatures responsible for the deterioration of the buildings. But, once the crowd had dispersed after the prayers were over, they had so many other things to think about that they forgot problems of hygiene.

"And for a start, it's all very well for Imam Rabah, but he seems to be forgetting that the water shortages are making our lives a misery! Then again, the blocks of flats and streets don't even belong to us! We're not going to clean up anything belonging to the government! You must be joking!"

ON THE THIRD FLOOR of the block of flats at number 13 Ramdane-Kahlouche Street, in the bedroom, on the bed, Boualem's body shudders as if he were receiving electric shocks. The regular features of his face are tense. The young man turns over several times, then he scrabbles for a cushion, crushes it against his head, and tries to stuff his ears with it—hopeless protection given the all-invasive sound of the loudspeaker broadcasting Imam Rabah's sermon. In so doing, he knocks the enormous antediluvian alarm clock off the chair where it was perched. The clatter completely awakens Boualem. Beside himself with rage, he hurls the pillow violently against the wall and sits up, his eyes swollen through broken sleep. Instinctively his hand gropes for the pack of cigarettes on the chair. His fingers tremble as he feverishly lights a match. He inhales a lungful of smoke from his strong cigarette and with the back of his hand wipes away the perspiration streaming from his forehead. Then he stubs out his cigarette in the rusty ashtray, gets up, jumps out of bed, puts on his denim jacket, and goes out, slamming the door.

It takes him a few minutes to climb the three stories, dodge through the deserted laundry room, and emerge on the terrace. He marches toward the loudspeaker lashed to a sturdy steel pole cemented to the parapet of the terrace. Here the voice of the Imam is even louder. The pliers Boualem is clutching in his hand whip out like a bird of prey and seize the wire round the loud-speaker just as the Imam is at the height of his frenzy. Boualem pays no heed. He snatches violently at the wire, twisting it back and forth, hurts his hand, then, without bothering about the blood flowing from his thumb, grabs the loudspeaker now freed from the wire and tears it away. The Imam's voice can no longer be heard. The only sound is the continuous moaning of the wind. Pleased with himself, Boualem sucks his thumb.

He glances up suddenly and meets the gaze of a girl watching him from behind the curtain in the window of the block of flats next door. Yamina is wearing a gray headscarf pulled down to cover her forehead and that completely hides her hair. Sensing she has been seen, she disappears behind the curtain. Boualem stops in his tracks, his eyes fixed to the window. He hopes Yamina will reappear. Only the twitching of the curtain indicates that the girl is still there. Boualem smiles, then picks up the loudspeaker while the distant voice of the Imam continues its increasingly heated diatribes, now lambasting the content of the television news the evening before. Boualem, upset at having been seen by Yamina, stuffs the pliers into his jacket pocket and covertly glances once more at the window. The curtain is now still. With the loud-speaker under his arm, he hurriedly leaves the terrace.

Yamina reappears. She looks at the pole to which the loud-speaker had been attached until a few moments before. She does not appear to understand the significance of the act Boualem has just committed.

When Boualem scrambles down the steps he is suddenly frightened by the realization of what he has done: the whole thing has not lasted more than five minutes. All at once his heart starts beating wildly and his face becomes livid. He stops dead, knowing that if he takes another step something will explode inside him. It is vital for him to control his breathing. Standing with his back against the wall, on the landing between two stories, he is anx-iously waiting to recover so he can set off again as soon as possi-ble. Finally his heartbeats calm down. The color returns to his face. Carefully, without hurrying, Boualem goes down the last few stairs to his apartment. He opens the door, checks there is no one there, goes to his room, puts the loudspeaker on the mattress, and sits down.

"Why on earth? Why?"

He does not dare to look directly at the bulky object on his bed. He checks for a minute or two to make sure that the "strange thing" that just visited him has truly disappeared. This "thing," which always descends upon him when he is least expecting it, batters his brain and makes his life a misery.

Fortunately it doesn't last long!

2

ROCHER CARRÉ, OR SQUARE ROCK, IS THE NAME GIVEN TO FOUR IMmense concrete blocks by the sea set in a line of large rocks forming a natural dike. It is here, not far away from Bab el-Oued, that many of the young men from this neighborhood and from the Casbah meet every day. With no one to bother them they are free to catch sewer fish, to doze lulled by the waves beating against the rocks, to discreetly drink their bottle of red wine, roll joints of hashish, or swallow a few Valium. There are two beaches with gray sand and stinking water on either side of this spot: Sandy Beach, otherwise known as the Horse Dip (because it used to be where they washed the donkeys that collected the rubbish from the Casbah), and Paradise Beach, also nicknamed Paralice Beach, at the bottom of the Bologhine neighborhood that used to be called Saint Eugène. The sky is bright blue, the sea fairly calm, and Rocher Carré seems crushed, wiped out by the heat.

A few skinny, suntanned children wearing oversized heavily darned underpants hanging down to their knees bravely cram together on an outcrop of rock forming a natural diving board. They jostle one another and dive awkwardly into the sea, one after the other, with loud shrieks and laughter. Other kids, just as young but pretending to be serious, untroubled by the boisterous behavior of the divers, are fishing, their fingers tightly gripping the end of their fishing rods. Their thin outstretched arms are no thicker than the cane they are holding. They keep a close watch on the waves slapping their feet, aware of the slightest movement that might mean a mullet or a sewer eel.

Then there are the teenagers, more imaginative, perched on large inner tubes from trucks or tractors, who let themselves be rocked by the swell of the sea. They seem to be dreaming of being whisked off to the faraway places where their vessels might take them. Some of them, To personalize their homemade lifebuoys, some of them have painted on them the names of some of the big cities figuring in their escapist dreams: London, Paris, Stockholm, and even Manchester United in a tribute to the famous English football team.

Boualem arrives nonchalantly toting a bulky sports bag. The harsh sound of a wailing siren makes him jump. He can't help it.

In the distance, on the boulevard, a police car races toward the district of Bologhine. Boualem climbs the rocks and walks to one of the four large concrete blocks. He gets as close as he can to the edge, looks round to make sure no one is watching, opens the bag, takes out the loudspeaker, and hurls it into the sea. It soon disappears, leaving a swirl of foam on the surface of the water. Boualem watches the waves for a few moments, then sits down on the rock and lights a cigarette.

"My God! What on earth made me do that?"

In the distance a young boy shouts excitedly since he has just caught a large fish. He tries to take out the hook with the help of his pals. Boualem thinks fleetingly of his younger brother Kader, an expert in fishing conger eels. Kader, without a care in the world.

Just when Boualem is getting ready to leave, his attention is drawn to a group of older boys he had not noticed when he arrived. The three adolescents are ensconced in a hollow of the rock where no one can see them. Wearing cheap imported Moroccan jeans, their shoulders protected from the sun by faded old T-shirts and with worn-out Adidas tennis shoes on their feet (those famous ones stolen from a depot during the October riots and distributed by the rioters among the youngsters of Bab el-Oued), Tahar, Karim, and Ali, their eyes half-closed, smiling and foolish, are inhaling the smoke from their joints, listening with half an ear to the rai music coming from Tahar's Sony ghetto-blaster. Deep in their fantasy world, light-years away from Bab el-Oued, they don't hear Boualem approaching along the immense esplanade. A few years before there had been an enormous stadium there called Marcel-Cerdan Stadium, later renamed Ferhani Stadium; it had then been demolished for some obscure reason. Tahar sees him first. He opens an eye. "Hi Boualem! How's it going?"

Boualem stops and puts down his empty bag. "Hi, Tahar! Hi Ali! Hi Karim! Still lazing about?"

He has seen at a glance that the three of them are high as kites on that wretched cheap shit whose sales have rocketed since the border with Morocco was opened: a mixture of bad grass, resin, and crushed neuroleptics. Enough to drive even the strongest crazy. He knows that Tahar, Karim, and Ali do almost nothing other than get high all day long. The rest of the time they go downtown to lift a few necklaces and wallets.

Boualem knows them well. Nice kids who didn't stand a chance. He has seen them grow up and go under. He knows they can no longer be rescued from their daily degradation. Anyway, who would want to save them?

Ali, who lives on the second floor of the same block of flats as he does, at 13 Ramdane-Kahlouche Street, is the one he knows best. A baby face who now looks twice his age, Ali has tried it all: glue sniffing, soft bread stuck to car exhaust pipes, resin, wax, fermented watermelon, ether. Any old combination, as long as it "makes you high and shoots you into another world."

Boualem remembers that horrible night he found Ali sprawling in a filthy municipal dump, the lower part of his body covered in blood. Ali had spent the day getting high, as desperate as a starving person craving food. Then he had become obsessed by an idée fixe: to become old. Immediately. He could no longer understand the point of being young and even less of having a prick. What was the use of virility when living a nonlife, like his? A recurrent nightmare. He decided to remove the useless piece of flesh. To beat it to a pulp with a piece of rock. To crush this ridiculous symbol found in every sentence but which, as far as he was concerned, was only used for peeing.

Boualem remembered the stunned looks of the nurses in the Central Hospital when he brought Ali in, unconscious and covered in blood. They immediately called the police and Boualem was subjected to lengthy and unpleasant questioning because they suspected him of unnatural sexual acts.

Ali was cared for. A female psychologist came to see him and took notes. He had absolutely nothing to tell her. The tranquilizers prescribed by the doctors made him feel better. He was still convinced that his sexual organ was no longer there. He had just had his sixteenth birthday. When Ali saw Boualem after leaving the hospital, he thanked him, though he said he would have preferred to have been left to rot in the rubbish dump.

They had never again talked of that dreadful night.

Boualem looks tenderly at Ali. Karim lifts his bony arms to the sky and stretches himself as if he had just woken up. "Relax! We're helping Ali count the days till he has to go into the army."

"Congratulations! It'll make a man of you," jokes Boualem gently, immediately regretting the trivial remark about something so significant for Ali.

Ali draws lazily on his cigarette. "Don't worry. With my luck I'm bound to end up in a disciplinary battalion near Béchar."

Karim adds in his husky voice, "He never stops going on about his disciplinary battalion."

Boualem picks up his bag. "Perhaps you'll find yourself in a cushy job in some ministerial department. The barracks are overcrowded just at the moment."

Karim snatches the cigarette from Ali. "We shouldn't be smoking these. They're only for the children of the rich."

"He'd be better off in Béchar; he'd be able to make a few quick trips to Morocco and bring us back the real thing," sighs Tahar, before closing his eyes and plunging once again into his dreams.

Boualem smiles at the three teenagers. "You'd do better to stop all this crap. It's pure poison you're smoking."

"We know. It's a better trip with this mixture though. You get as high as the moon."

"Well, I'm off. Watch out now."

Boualem gives a friendly wave and goes on his way wondering for the nth time how he, steeped just like all the kids he knows in this sordid universe, has managed to escape the artificial paradise. He can't understand why he rejected it. "Unless it was divine protection. Thank God for that."

3

NIGHT HAS FALLEN IN BAB EL-OUED. THE STREETS ARE QUIETER now. A few cars race along the boulevards. Most of the shop fronts have been padlocked and the blinds pulled down. The streets are scarcely lit, if at all. For years Algiers has come to a standstill after nightfall. In the squares with the stunted trees and in the entrances to blocks of flats, young men driven outdoors by the heat and the overcrowding indoors get together and talk, sometimes until dawn.

Some groups are mainly made up of young men with beards who, garbed in their white or gray *qamis,* are the most vehement, spending hours philosophizing about the miraculous discovery of a hot water well in the middle of the ocean by Jacques Cousteau or about the conversion to Islam of Cat Stevens or Maurice Béjart.

In a cul-de-sac there is a small bakery with an alluring name: *The Flower of Bab el-Oued.* The shelves in the window are laden with artificially colored cream cakes. A little notice says "At the Flower of Bab el-Oued, you can find the best bread in Algiers, the Islamic world, and the African Continent."

The bakery is bursting with activity. Boualem, stripped to the waist, is putting in the oven the loaves of bread that Mabrouk, the young baker's-boy, lines up on the wooden shovel. Bent over the bread sorter at the other end of the bakery is Hassan the proprietor, a magnificent specimen of a fifty-year-old. He has lively eyes, is wearing impeccably white Italian-style trousers, and is very laid back, his paunch wobbling as he moves busily around his machine. His deft movements are swift and regular.

"Come on, lads! Get a move on! Mustn't fall asleep now. We'll be on croissants in twenty minutes' time. It's nearly daylight. Hello there, Mabrouk! Up in the clouds again? Dreaming of life back home in Paris I expect."

Mabrouk, a heavyset twenty-two-year-old with a jolly chubby-cheeked face covered in spots and blackheads, answers by pulling a face. Wearing headphones attached to the Walkman on his belt, his sophisticated haircut and black mittens with a red star on his left hand make him look vaguely like those young blacks from the Bronx or like the new rappers you see on the videoclips broadcast by the satellite television channels. He too is bare-chested and sweating profusely. Hassan teases him once again. "Dreaming of Belsunce or Barbès, are we?"

"That's one time too many!" mutters Chubby Cheeks, taking off his headphones.

"Did you notice that even with his headphones on he can hear what I am saying? As soon as we mention Marseilles or Barbès he sits up." The muezzin's voice calls the faithful to the dawn prayer. Hassan shakes his flour-covered hands. "Already? Alright, I'm off!"

He disappears into the back of the bakery to carry out his ablutions before the prayers.

Mabrouk whispers to Boualem, "I don't like Hassan's bullshit. Sometimes he really pisses me off. I'm not fifteen anymore."

"Forget it! He's only teasing. You know he's fond of you."

Mabrouk smoothes his hair with the back of his hand. An automatic gesture: his gel-coated locks are all in place.

"Yeah! But he does go on. And I don't like it."

Boualem pulls out a packet of cigarettes from his jeans jacket and lights up. Mabrouk watches him out of the corner of his eye. "You don't look too good tonight."

Boualem puffs thoughtfully at his cigarette. "It's nothing much. I think I've done something stupid."

"Not too serious I hope. What was it?" asks Mabrouk, really curious.

"Ah, forget it!"

Disappointed, Mabrouk replaces his headphones and takes some chewing tobacco out of his pocket.

He makes a quid for himself while secretly watching Boualem. Hassan, finished washing, has returned with a towel round his neck. He pretends to disapprove of Mabrouk when he places the quid inside his lower lip.

"I hope it won't end up in the dough for the croissants."

Mabrouk sways his head in time to the music he is supposed to be listening to. He laughs to himself.

"Shit! This new one from Public Enemy is great."

Hassan pretends to be disgusted. He unfurls a small carpet and begins the prayer. Boualem suppresses a giggle and he too leaves the bakery to perform his ablutions. The tap is turned on once again.

4

A new day dawns in Bab el-Oued. The sky is blue, cloudless; it almost looks as if the clammy layer of pollution usually hanging over the city has followed the clouds of sand on their long trip north.

A shape completely covered with a sheet is stretched out on Boualem's bed. Suddenly, like a fury, Hanifa bursts into the room. Tall and heavily built, she inspires fear and authority with her muscular arms, broad hips, and large, still-firm breasts swinging loose beneath her yellow-flowered Kabyle dress. The curlers she wears every day make you feel she is always about to participate in some ceremony or other, a wedding, engagement, or circumcision, whereas in fact she never goes out at all.

The only place outdoors where she is frequently to be found is the terrace, three stories above the apartment. This is where all the major household tasks take place: washing sheets, beating carpets, stuffing mattresses, and preparing tripe. A place for her and all the other women living in the building who regularly meet there to avoid suffocation.

Hanifa, Boualem's eldest sister, knows she has got to be able to cope, because ever since their parents died she has been in charge of the family. She still cannot understand why tuberculosis afflicted their family. Since the 1940s this vile disease, the enemy of the poor, had devastated them. Of the fourteen children, only

Kader, Boualem, and Hanifa herself have survived. She thinks of Mohammed, her eldest brother—so handsome and so considerate—struck down in 1958 at the age of twenty. As hardworking and considerate as Boualem.

Their father and mother had contracted the disease first, and, unknowing, continued procreating. They kept going despite the germs lurking in the damp rooms, which slipped into the bodies of the newborn babies. It was an annual challenge to death. They almost always lost, but never gave up.

Toward the end of the 1960s the right drugs finally appeared. At that time the family lived in a run-down block of flats in Celestial Village, a neighborhood above Notre Dame d'Afrique, the "negro village," as the French settlers called it. Hanifa and her mother had become regulars at the social health dispensary in Bab el-Oued. There was nothing wrong with the girl though. Her lungs were intact. But since she was the sole survivor, her mother protected her like the apple of her eye, stuffing her with Rumifon, the new miracle product, despite protests from the social workers and the nuns. The drug made the little girl double in size. Her mother was pleased. "When people see you now, they won't be able to say that's the family with consumption."

As for their father, his treatment was stuffing himself with tomatoes. A cure straight from the village.

Kader and Boualem were born in the Bab el-Oued apartment, after Independence when the disease had disappeared. Boualem's appearance was the symbol of the family's renewed happiness. The father spent two months completely repainting the apartment with several coats of whitewash. "A boy who won't have tuberculosis! May Allah be praised for his goodness . . ." A huge couscous was prepared and shared among the poor of Sidi Abderrahman.*

Kader's birth, a few years later, was an accident that was an inconvenience to all because of the lack of space in the flat, but "*Katba!* What is written is written." He just had time to get to know his parents, who were carried off within a few months of one another by a kidney infection and acute hypertension.

Whenever Hanifa remembered the bad times of tuberculosis she broke out in a cold sweat.

"Praise the Lord! Our family might have been exterminated."

Boualem, a hardworking decent boy, went out to work very young. For the moment, brother and sister were jointly in charge.

---

*The patron saint of Algiers.

Boualem, outside the house, with a wage "coming in each month," and Hanifa inside, responsible for running it. Of course, there was also the monthly alimony she received from her bastard of an ex-husband since her divorce.

Hanifa, with a sigh, returns to present reality. She unceremoniously whips off the sheet, uncovering her brother Kader, a pale puny boy huddled in his white *gandoura*. She shakes him and shouts at him in her sergeant major's voice, "Come on, Kader, time to get up! It's seven o'clock. Your brother Boualem is back already . . . Up you get! Up you get!"

Kader sits up, his eyes puffy with sleep. "What's the matter now! School only starts at ten o'clock."

"That's not my problem! I need to get the bed ready for your brother. If you really want to go back to sleep you can go into my room: just don't wake up the twins. Come on, get a move on!"

He gets up, grumbling. "It's always the same. And I don't want to sleep with the twins. Their bed smells of sick."

Hanifa moves through the room like a fury. "I'll give you sick, I will! Out you go! I'm having a thorough cleanup today anyway!"

Before leaving the room he collects his clothes scattered at the foot of the bed. "You'll miss me when I clear off to Canada!"

"That'll be the day! In the meantime, go and wash your face."

Kader, with a swish of his *gandoura,* gets out quickly. Hanifa opens the window, chases away her gloomy thoughts, and swiftly remakes the bed. She smiles, happy, when all is said and done, to be living in the company of her two brothers and her own twins. She considers herself a queen amongst these men who love her and whom she loves. And then again she feels so much affection for Kader, her little brother, despite his complicated nature, his poor school results, his addiction to sleeping late in the mornings and to having siestas!

5

I N THE BLOCK OF FLATS NEXT DOOR, AT NUMBER 15 RAMDANE-Kahlouche Street, a new day is about to begin. Saïd is in the tiny family bathroom (a cubbyhole, scarcely larger than a cupboard). In front of the mirror, with sullen gaze and luxuriant beard, he is delicately applying a line of kohl along his eyelid. He blinks, then deals with his other eye. He can't prevent his face tensing up despite his best efforts. Saïd feels that if he doesn't control himself he might explode, do something dreadful.

That's just the way it is. He can't help it. Ever since the loud-speaker disappeared he has been seething with rage. An incomprehensible act. Outrageous. An obvious act of provocation, deliberately aimed at him, he who had so carefully taken charge of installing all the loudspeakers in the neighborhood. And now here was a "monster," a lackey of Satan who had dared . . . For the last two days Saïd has been falling asleep and waking up obsessed by the burning question of who could possibly be guilty of this act of sacrilege beyond all reason.

Having finished his delicate task, he rinses out his mouth, spits into the washbasin, then leaves the bathroom. He strides down the dark corridor whose walls are covered with illuminated religious manuscripts brought back from pilgrimages to Saudi Arabia. As he walks, Saïd enjoys making lots of noise with his plastic Puma flip-flops.

He crosses a room that is used as a sitting–cum–dining room. This is where Lalla Jamila, his mother, spends her days, bent over her Singer sewing machine, making school overalls for a Mozabite retailer who sells them in his shop in Lyre Street. This morning the sewing machine is still at rest, under its cover, waiting for Lalla Jamila to finish preparing the meal.

Saïd draws back a curtain and goes out onto the balcony. Yamina, scarf on her head, very beautiful with her gentle face and large sad eyes, a *hidjab* covering her body down to the ankles, is hanging out the washing. Despite the wide shapeless garment, one can just discern the lines of her body. She jumps when Saïd yells at her, "Does it take you a whole morning to hang out the washing?"

Yamina moves away. "You're not going to start this early in the morning."

"That's what you think! Who's to stop me!" He grabs her by the tunic and shakes her violently. She drops the shirt she was about to hang up.

"You spend your days at the window or parading around this shitty balcony and I'm not supposed to say anything?" He shoves her against the wall.

"Stop it, you're hurting me."

"There'll soon be a wall just here. No more balcony. You'll see what an Islamic *hadjib* really means." Saïd glares inquisitorially at his sister. "In the meantime we need to have a little talk. Since you're always poking your nose outside perhaps you might happen to have seen who it was who stole the loudspeaker."

Yamina is used to the daily attacks of her brother, but suddenly she is completely thrown by this last sentence, panic-stricken at the idea that he might suspect Boualem. Why is he asking her this? What exactly does he know? The only defense Yamina uses is immediate retort. She shoves Saïd away. "Just who do you think you are? Don't you touch me!"

She grabs the aluminum basin which contained the washing and brandishes it like a weapon. "You'd better not get any closer!"

Saïd says sarcastically, "You think I'm scared of you?"

Hearing the shouting, Lalla Jamila hurries outside. She is used to the endless quarrelling between Saïd and his sister and intervenes somewhat unconvincingly. She speaks to her son as if she were addressing a naughty child. "Off you go again! And on the balcony what's more! To keep the neighbors amused I suppose . . . Bravo! Clear off! Inside with you."

Matching gesture to words, she grabs Saïd and unceremoniously bundles him into the apartment. "Can't you find anything better to do than annoy your sister?"

"There we go! You're always on her side. If you only knew what she was thinking, that little hypocrite."

"Just you leave her alone. That's all."

Yamina, feeling protected, changes her tone. "This coward hasn't yet met anyone who will put him in his place."

"D'you hear how she speaks to me? And last Friday instead of being in the mosque who knows what she got up to."

Yamina slips behind her mother. "Why don't you ask your informers who spend their time spying on girls?"

Lalla Jamila, firm and decisive, adjusts her flowered headscarf and pushes Saïd toward the corridor. "Right! Now, Saïd, go away and let us do the housework!"

He stops and, hands on hips, faces up to the two women. "Sooner or later I'll sort out this household! I'm the one in charge here! Ever since my father died, God rest his soul, this place has been going downhill."

He looks resentfully one last time at his sister, then beats a retreat.

Lalla Jamila, thinking of the work awaiting her, goes to the sewing machine and removes its cover.

"All right, all right! You bring back a wage and then you can be in charge."

Yamina cannot suppress a mocking smile before she returns to the balcony. The front door slams violently.

WHEN SAÏD, ANNOYED, runs down the stairway of the flats, he is convinced that things will go his way in the end. His mother and sister will not go on being the only ones who don't respect him; everyone else in the whole neighborhood admires him unreservedly. Even those in other neighborhoods nearby. And quite right too.

Unemployed, a layabout since being thrown out of primary school, Saïd was an obscure reject of the neighborhood for years until fame suddenly descended upon him one day in October 1988. That particular morning he happened to be bravely positioned in the front line of the rioters from Bab el-Oued. Like all the other young men, he had revolt in his guts. His hatred for the state, the administration, the police, for villas, shops, company cars, banks, trains, airplanes was so strong that he thoroughly enjoyed destruction, deeply loved smashing things, looting, burning cars, erecting barricades, and ended up, as a dangerous ringleader, in the hands of the police, who made him round off his epic adventures as riot leader in a suburban police station. He spent more than a fortnight there "helping the police with their inquiries." He got out thanks to the amnesty, covered in the flamboyant glory of the popular hero, and became the unchallenged star of Bab el-Oued. Much more famous than Madjer, the most popular football player of the moment.

It was mainly his courageous resistance to torture that established his reputation. He enjoyed telling everyone about this resistance, using hundreds of details each more horrible than the last. In the gloomy police cell between two bouts of "questioning" he had discovered religious faith. He liked to compare this lightning conversion to that of the famous Ali sharp-fingers, an ex-thug turned hero then martyr of urban guerrilla warfare during the liberation struggle and whose adventures he had followed in the film *The Battle of Algiers,* which had had a runaway success at the Marignan cinema.

The episode he liked best, to make his mates shudder and fire their imagination, was the one where the policeman who had been beaten up by the rioters a few days previously had in revenge placed Saïd's balls in a drawer, then slammed it shut. "Hell! Help! Mother!" In a fraction of a second Saïd "had visited hell, the galaxies, the black hole." Since no one could decently ask to see the results of this atrocious torture, they had to take his word for it. His reputation as a hero did the rounds of the popular neighborhoods and the football stadiums when there were important matches.

Not long after that he started assiduously attending the Hayat mosque, met the major religious leaders, and initiated himself into verbal extremism, for want of anything better to do.

Obviously he let his beard grow and started wearing the *qamis*, though he did not get rid of the black leather jacket he was particularly fond of: it reminded him of the cold evenings in the past when he went home after sipping a few beers. "A time I am ashamed of. Luckily Allah has shown me the right path."

The militants of Bab el-Oued knew they could count on him. A good recruit. Not much brain, but disciplined and possessing a certain stature and personality, which made their mark. After a month's training he was given a few tasks organizing and mobilizing the young. That was how he had become the most popular personality of the suburb of Bab el-Oued and the surrounding area. Yet they, his mother and sister, dared to stand up to him!

Pondering these thoughts, Saïd walks past the Flower of Bab el-Oued without slowing down.

6

BEHIND HIS COUNTER, HASSAN THE BAKER IS IN GOOD SHAPE DESPITE the night he has spent in the bakery. He is bursting with health. "May Allah keep the Evil Eye and the jealous away from here!" The baker's shop, just like every morning, is crammed with clients jostling one another to buy bread, croissants, pizzas . . . A habit due to fear of shortages.

An old client, who looks straight out of a television sketch, ensconced in a blue suit and with his head covered in an Istanbul headscarf such as you almost never see in Algiers nowadays, leans against a shelf, eats a slice of piping hot pizza while cynically observing the pushing and shoving in the shop.

"Heavens above! You'd think they were dying of hunger! My word, they're going to clear out the shop! If we ever run out of bread one day we'll just eat each other up, and that's that!"

Hassan gently reproves him: "Aami Mourad! Leave my clients alone. No need to push, there'll be enough for everyone at the Flower of Bab el-Oued! The best bread in the Third World!"

Aami Mourad swallows another bite of pizza and wipes his mouth. "Hey there, baker! Seems there's going to be a flour strike next week. What are these poor people going to eat then? Eh? Can you tell me that? The best baker in the Third World . . ."

Hassan smoothes his moustache and doesn't respond to the provocation. This particular morning, just like each morning that God has given for the last few years, he is not really dissatisfied with himself. A patient but perceptible success.

Starting with nothing, he now owns a shop. His family is catered for and, furthermore, healthwise, everything is fine. "Thank the Lord." He just ought to decide to get around to doing a few exercises to lose his spare tire. A simple life. What more could you want? A bit of excitement? So what!

The famous atmosphere of Bab el-Oued in the 1950s . . . Images that sometimes haunt him and are part of a distant past. When he was young.

His being part of Bab el-Oued is a gut feeling since he is fully aware that there are not many people who can boast, as he can, of being true Babelouedians. He was born and bred there, at a time when the neighborhood was almost exclusively occupied by the French settlers. Then there were none of those "backwoodsmen from the mountains with their *chechias* who came down from their plateaux after Independence" and who these days are busy showing off, putting on drawling affected accents, wearing revolutionaries' clothes, black sandals, telling everyone to piss off and passing themselves off as homegrown locals. No! Hassan is not one of those. He is proud of being one of the chosen few with the memory of the district engraved in his heart.

He knows and loves this district well, mainly because of its splendor and glory of yesteryear . . . When the smell of grilled merguez sausages, sardines in esquabeche, anisette, and tramousses would tickle your nostrils on Sunday mornings, with, as a bonus, the waves of bracing sea air wafting from the coast . . . When the burning rays of the sun scorched the bare shoulders of the girls who swarmed around Grosoli's ice cream kiosk to buy their cornets . . . Hassan cannot think of this past without thinking bitterly and resentfully of the present and its mixture of dull everyday existence and progressive deterioration. And the smells! Apart from the sacred period of Ramadan during which the scents of spices, chorba, mint, and orange flower water perfume the streets, it is mainly the stinking open sewers that predominate.

That is why, this particular morning, if Hassan is acknowledging that he is happy and congratulating himself at having a calm and well-filled life, it is perhaps because he feels he should, because it is the beginning of the week and because being optimistic wards off the Evil Eye. In fact, it is obvious there is something not quite right in his life, in the neighborhood, and in the country. Something is wrong. "I could even say that quite a lot of things are not quite right."

As a consolation he tries to convince himself that compared to others, who can't even afford to fill up their shopping baskets, he can't complain, but nonetheless his Algeria has changed an awful lot. So he'd better to get down to work rather than carrying on about it and making it worse by chewing over this resentment and these insidious thoughts which are, there is no doubt about it, the work of the Evil one who perniciously distills the poison of despair in the minds of decent people.

7

THE WINDOW OF ONE OF THE APARTMENTS ON THE FIFTH FLOOR OF 15 Ramdane-Kahlouche Street opens to reveal Didine, barely awake, a cup of coffee in his hand. His skeletal body covered in a kind of African *jellaba* seems suspended, ready to fly away at the merest breath of wind. The young man's red hair, almost auburn because of the henna he has put on it, is quite dazzling when a ray of sunlight catches it. A dishevelled head of hair, because Didine hasn't taken the trouble to comb it before having his early morning cup of coffee. He blinks his eyes in the bright light.

He swallows a mouthful of coffee and delicately spits out a tiny piece of chick pea, which should not have been in his cup. Didine is not too fussy; he knows that the way things are at the moment he might well find anything in his coffee: the blends produced by the coffee roasters are ingenious. Anything that might provide the illusion of drinking a real strong black coffee—ground olive stones, chick peas, lentils—is used. The main thing is to avoid breaking a tooth in the process.

In the block of flats opposite, Didine glimpses the blonde voluptuous Lynda whose face is dotted with moles, chewing her eternal chewing gum. Leaning out of her window she is pulling up a piece of string attached to a book with a battered cover and yellowing pages, whose title, *Fiery Passion,* makes Didine's eyes pop open. Two floors below, another young girl, also leaning out of her window, is anxiously following the slow progression of the book. Lynda, her body arched and muscles taut, is doing her best to control the string and prevent the book from swinging too much.

"Did you enjoy it?"

Skinny Hannane raises her thin voice to make herself heard.

"You can't imagine! I've been crying for two days. Especially when Vito and Jolanda get together again."

"Great! Next week I'll be getting another: *Hannah, or the Whims of Passion.* You'll really love it."

Didine hasn't missed a word of this conversation between the two girls. He yells out, "Hey Lynda! I haven't read that one. Could I rent it off you?"

LYNDA HAS BECOME the darling of the neighborhood ever since she discovered a small market niche that enables her to earn some pocket money easily, without even leaving the building. She rents out books that her sailor cousin brings back from abroad. "Fifty-fifty share of profits!" A network of her women friends has been set up. The books are now happily circulating. People are falling over themselves for them. Top of the list is the Harlequin collection.

"Didine! I've already told you that what you ought to be reading are good thrillers, S.A.S. style, with gun battles and murders. You seem to be forgetting you're a man," answers Lynda sarcastically.

"But Lynda! You know I hate violence. I love wonderful romantic stories which set you dreaming. Like in *Falcon Crest*." He begins declaiming in an effeminate voice the dialogues of an American soap, mimicking the voices of the characters. The girls burst out laughing. Lynda, carried away by her fits of laughter, lets the string slip. The book falls into the street. The two young women cry out simultaneously.

"Shit! The book!"

In the space of a few seconds a child who happened to be on the pavement grabs it and disappears.

"The little devil! He stole it! I recognized him. He's Yamina's brother."

Didine crows with pleasure. "Serves you right! God is punishing you."

Lynda looks daggers at him. "Piss off. You limp-wristed fairy!"

She slams the window shut, immediately followed by Hannane. Didine, pleased with himself, closes his, then opens it suddenly and shouts, imitating the famous perfume advertisement: "Egoïste, Egoïste!"

"You old fairy!" yells Lynda at him from behind the glass.

Didine doesn't feel he is a fairy at all. He's simply effeminate and to be noticed he enhances this to be deliberately provocative. It is true that he has always enjoyed being in women's company and taking part in their conversations. That doesn't bother anyone because he almost never goes out. He has been very affected by the recent death of his grandmother, of whom he was very fond, and has been depressed ever since the funeral. She was the one who looked after him and brought him up. He spent his child-hood under her wing. When he was a teenager he realized that he talked like his grandmother, that he was very like her. The only problem was that he could not, as she did, wear the traditional veil.

8

HANIFA, BOUALEM'S SISTER, AND OTHER WOMEN, YOUNG AND OLD, are out very early on the terrace of 13 Ramdane-Kahlouche Street. They try to make the most of the cool part of the day be-fore the noon furnace turns the tiles into hot coals. Between 7 and 11:30 in the morning, according to a strict rota, they do the washing, hang it out, beat the mattresses, and, if they've enough time, wash themselves or get the children to take baths in the shared utility room.

The terrace is the mythical place where news and gossip are exchanged. It belongs exclusively to the popular democratic as-sembly of the women living in the building. It is their little bit of shared universe. Except for the day Saïd and the militants went up there to put up the loudspeaker, no man ever goes there because of the *horma*. Hanifa is the life and soul of the group. She is always the one who starts off and keeps the conversations going.

"If I were in the government and had to deal with the 'eco-nomic crisis,' as they call it, I would suggest we sell Bab el-Oued. The whole neighborhood, just as it is. The women on the terraces, the men in the streets, the teenagers propping up the walls. They could put it on show at Madame Tussaud's museum in London and it would bring us in some foreign currency."

Having established the subject, the discussion starts off imme-diately. Each woman expresses her viewpoint.

"I dunno! D'you think the English'd like it? I get the feeling we don't interest anyone anymore."

"The only thing that would save the country would be if they sold us women like they used to."

"They could line us up naked on the Place des Trois Horloges and auction us off."

"I wonder how much I'd be worth?"

Hanifa bursts out laughing. "You? It's not a body you've got there, it's a bag of bones. Not even ten dinars, if you ask me. My God! If I could only meet a handsome prince from the Gulf, or a Swiss banker."

"You're a bit long in the tooth for that! Even your one-eyed wheeler-dealer husband left you."

Hanifa, pretending to be offended, throws a wet pullover in the woman's face. "*Bouh'alik!* You must be joking! I was the one that left him, that good-for-nothing! I'd much rather be on my own with my family than doing the cooking and housework in his nouveau riche villa for his whole tribe of peasants."

Hanifa is surprised to find herself thinking back over the few months she spent in the "nearly finished" villa belonging to her son-of-a-bitch husband. A crafty, one-eyed, potbellied wheeler-dealer who got rich quick thanks to the famous scam they had of importing European cows in the 1980s. Hanifa recognized that her marriage had been arranged. She admitted she was no longer a fresh young girl and was handicapped when she got married by coming from a poor family. What she could not accept was that by marrying her, her vile crook of an ex-husband had acquired a cleaning woman as well as the bonus of free sex at home, saving himself expensive tedious escapades in a covered truck: bachelor outings every weekend to visit the whores living in the large state tourist complexes.

The famous villa of the wheeler-dealer-spouse had three stories, was supposed to be in Spanish style—a hacienda like in Mexico—and was repulsively ugly. Because it was a never-ending building site, each morning Hanifa had to sweep up sand and cement, and, to cap it all, had to put up with the oppressive presence of his five brothers. All unmarried, clumsy oafs, each one more devious than his brothers, with a vague, defective view of hygiene and social skills; since they had only recently left their plateaus to come and live in the city, they tended to mistake the large comfortable rooms of the villa for the stables where they spent so much time during their European cows escapade.

But what had pushed Hanifa into making the ultimate decision, a few months after the wedding, had been the strange idiosyncrasies of her mother-in-law, a respectable lady who had not understood the changes which had taken place in her life and had the annoying habit of confusing the toilet bowl with the bidet in the bathroom. Her most serious fault though was the ferocious hatred she had nursed toward Hanifa ever since the wedding night. A hatred she delighted in cultivating in the company of Ma M'barka, with whom she spent most of her time, an old bonesetter-witch from Chéraga who regularly provided her with concoctions to get her daughter-in-law to clear off as soon as possible. This is why Hanifa had unwittingly tasted all the different potions available in the country, and even some from Niger or Mali. One day she very nearly passed away after drinking a deadly soup in which the old lady had marinated poisonous Saharan cactus, chameleon liver, and cat gut.

That was the last straw for Hanifa, especially since she could no longer stand being raped every three days by her devious crook of a husband. In his youth he had never had an opportunity to discover the point of kisses or caresses, so his idea of loving tenderness, when he was feeling randy, was to yell at her, "Are you clean today?" Sometimes, though, he did like to show his affection, expressed by whacking her bottom unexpectedly when she passed by, a habit he had picked up in the brothel.

The fateful, happy, long-awaited day arrived. The suitcases were ready, lined up in the hallway of the villa, at the feet of the stoical Hanifa who had put on her *hidjab* and was standing with the twins in her arms, impatiently awaiting the arrival of her brother to collect her. Boualem bravely confronted the wheeler-dealer and his brothers who were unwilling to let their prey escape. The mother-in-law kept out of it and said her prayers.

Finally, after lengthy confabulations, the husband agreed to a divorce and to pay out a modest amount of alimony for the twins, since he was convinced his offspring would one day become cattle-breeders in "an Algeria which would come to understand its true vocation as an agricultural and dairy-farming country." In his heart of hearts he was not displeased because he was starting to miss the whores; particularly since he had learned that a few new stupendous nightclubs had opened, and especially the one in the Houbel district where you could rub shoulders nonstop till daybreak with the sons of the rich, with girl students out for the night, with artists and fellow piss-artists.

As for the mother-in-law, she was gleefully rubbing her hands at the successful outcome. She intended to go and see Ma M'barka as soon as possible to plan a new wedding for her son, with a young girl of eighteen solid as a rock and docile as a lamb. She had indeed already got her eye on one from the hammam.

Zohra pinches Hanifa's bottom. "Don't you get any ideas, Hanifa! You know that in our neighborhood there seems to be a curse on women: those who are married get divorced and the unmarried girls don't find husbands at all."

Hanifa says sarcastically, hand on hip, "Only natural! Now that the men spend their time talking politics or in the mosques."

"So they don't have time to bother with us. They're quite happy on their own."

"Yesterday I saw Arezki and Hamid. They were walking hand in hand."

"I rather like Arezki. I could eat him up and I'd start with his beard."

Hanifa happens to glance at the pole to which the loud-speaker had been attached. She frowns. "Hey! Have you noticed they've taken away the loudspeaker?"

Some of the women look over at the pole.

"Maybe they think the sermons of Imam Rabah aren't worth listening to."

"My husband told me it has been stolen!"

"I don't see who could steal it."

"We're the ones with the keys to the terrace."

"Thieves are mainly interested in satellite dishes."

Lynda erupts onto the terrace, clutching in her arms a batch of her steamy Harlequin series books. She bursts a bubble in her chewing gum with the tip of her tongue.

"Hello girls! I've got the latest collection here for those who are interested!"

She is immediately surrounded by a group of women. The books are handed around. Even those who can't read are interested; they know they'll be able to find a son or daughter who'll read to them. They feel there is something subversive about having books like this at home. They hide them under mattresses, in trunks, and the men do not know anything about it. "After all, they too have their secrets, outside the house in the bars and mosques!" The craziest month was when Lynda brought them several paperback copies of the famous *Kama Sutra*. The women loved it, decided to experiment with some of the suggestions and then report the results. A strange panic took hold of the terraces. The women spoke of nothing but sex.

"You don't happen to have seen Yamina? Her little brother has stolen one of my books," mentions Lynda casually, on her way toward the utility room.

The women, still busy handing around the books, do not answer.

"I'm going to have a bath. The heat is killing me! We're in luck, there's water this morning. Have you finished doing the washing?"

In the washhouse Lynda takes off her T-shirt, skirt, and pants. Near the washbasin an ingenious system for a homemade shower has been devised by the women. A pipe takes the water into a couscous pan fixed to the ceiling. The water comes out through the holes in the pan. Lynda makes no attempt to hide her body. She gets under the couscous pan and turns on the tap. The cold water makes her shiver. Her brown nipples harden and goose pimples appear in waves of electricity on her arms.

"The water is freezing. How wonderful!"

Aïcha, a girl of eighteen wearing a black headscarf and light-colored *hidjab,* is the only one taking any interest in Lynda's nakedness. She peeks at her through the slightly open door, then goes into the washroom and studies her.

"Why don't you close the door when you take a shower?"

Lynda is not surprised by Aïcha.

"Because I have nothing to hide . . ."

"Why not just admit you want them to look at you?"

Aïcha makes this comment in a voice tight with emotion. She pushes the door to and sits on the edge of the sink. She hoists up her *hidjab* to mid-thigh and takes out a packet of cigarettes from an inside pocket. Deftly she lights one and inhales deeply.

"Can I take a look at you?"

Lynda takes a few seconds to answer the question she was asked in a soft whisper. She looks Aïcha straight in the eyes, smiles at her, then her mouth parts slightly showing the tip of a small pink tongue, which licks the water streaming off her face.

"Of course! It's alright if you look at me . . . I know you enjoy it so much. You can even soap me in a minute."

Aïcha closes her eyes and lets her head tilt backward. Lynda secretly watches her while washing her breasts.

"But I would like you to stop being so jealous."

9

THE LITTLE SQUARE WITH THE CRUMBLING STONE BENCHES IS seething with movement. Saïd has convened a group of about twenty young men from the neighborhood. Leaning against a tree trunk in the middle, he spends a long time watching them to intimidate them, then raises his hand to impose silence. Among his followers, all bearded, all wearing *qamis* and leather jackets, Rashid stands out because of his Afghan beret. Messaoud, known as Mess, the émigré, is conspicuous because of his bandy legs. Saïd adopts a dogmatic tone while continuing to glare at those he is addressing.

"This is a very serious matter. The person who stole that loud-speaker wanted to put a stop to the voice of God. It's an attack on our religion. He shall be found. Make no mistake. This dreadful act is an attack on us all. You must help us. If you have any information you must pass it on to us. The thief will certainly try to sell it at the *dlala*. His act will be punished. God's judgment will be terrible."

Boualem with his sports bag over his shoulder appears at the end of the street. Lost in his thoughts, he does not notice the gathering. Saïd, though, has seen him, and follows his movements with dislike in his eyes. Rashid, who has picked that up, observes Saïd as Boualem disappears round the corner. Saïd, perhaps because of Boualem's brief appearance, becomes even more agitated. He starts haranguing the crowd and talks louder and louder:

"We shall clean up this neighborhood! There are too many im-moral things happening here each day. That woman, for instance, who lives alone and has men visit her at home. She wasn't even born here. She brings shame upon us. She should leave. We shall make her leave. We don't want any immoral people around here. Nonbelievers in our neighborhood . . ."

Rashid nods his approval of Saïd's words and adjusts his Afghan beret. Mess, who hasn't understood much, strokes his in-cipient beard.

"And one day, in this country, the Kalashnikovs will speak!"

The audience patiently awaits the end of the meeting. The young men, who know Saïd well, have noticed that today he is unusually tense. Sarcastic. That's why none of them dares to ask a question. Mess is the first to break the silence. He leans toward Saïd and speaks to him in a low voice, in French, with his strong Parisian accent.

"Hey, Saïd, I'm off, I've got to make a phone call."

Saïd, irritated by this untimely interruption, answers roughly in Arabic, "See you at the mosque, God willing . . ."

10

OUARDYA SLOWLY OPENS THE DOOR TO HER APARTMENT. HER FACE lights up when she sees Boualem.

"Hello, Ouardya!"

She moves aside and lets him in. She follows him into the enormous darkened living room.

"Hello! Did you manage to find some?"

Boualem gives her a pleased smile and points at the bag, which looks heavy.

"It's becoming more and more difficult, but I managed."

He looks at Ouardya, then glances at the heavily curtained window.

"You should open it. It's a beautiful sunny day, and the air . . ."

"No! I prefer not to. I haven't even got my makeup on . . ."

Boualem takes a seat and observes Ouardya with affection. Embarrassed, she bows her head. At forty, despite her strange thinness, the white streaks in her hair, and the countless tiny wrinkles on her face, Ouardya does not seem older than any other woman her age. Her large eyes, though heavily shadowed and badly bloodshot, are shining. There is a pathetic charm about her, perhaps because of her dark skin and a little blemish—a scar—on her right cheek, or perhaps simply because of the way she moves. As if she were gliding in the half-darkness. Or perhaps it comes from her voice whispering rather than speaking, for fear of upsetting a mysterious balance?

Boualem is deeply intimidated each time he goes to visit her. It is a feeling of bewilderment he can neither explain nor control. He too speaks softly. He would rather be silent and listen to Ouardya speak. She adjusts the folds of her old dressing gown and runs a hand through her hair.

"How much do I owe you?"

Boualem puts his bag on the table, opens it, and takes out some bottles of wine.

"It's gone up again. They really want to put people off drinking."

Ouardya smiles feebly. She glances at the bottles.

"D'you mind if I open one? I haven't had any since the day before yesterday."

"They're all for you. But what I'd like would be a glass of cold water."

"Of course!"

She moves to the table, takes hold of a bottle, and goes into the kitchen. On the way, she hesitates, then lightly touches Boualem's hair, a brief caress that makes him shiver.

"Thank you!" He smiles and blushes at the same time, lights a cigarette, and seems to be talking to himself since Ouardya is already in the kitchen.

"If my sister could see me . . . Supplying wine."

Ouardya, uncorking the bottle, has half heard him.

"What did you say?"

"No, nothing. I'm not going to be able to stay long."

He gets up and briskly zips up his bag. Ouardya reappears, clutching in her hand a glass of wine filled right to the brim. Boualem whistles. "You ought to go easy. Otherwise they won't last you long."

"I can't help it. It's so good!"

Ouardya swallows a little mouthful, closes her eyes, and smacks her lips. Boualem watches her, deep in thought. Wherever does he get this urge to advise people about what is good or bad? Ouardya moves toward him. "Are you leaving?"

"Yes!"

She looks at him. Her lips part slightly but the words don't come out. She merely smiles sadly, then her hand slowly approaches his face. She strokes his cheek. Boualem grasps her hand and kisses it.

"I like coming to see you. Because it's . . . I don't know . . . It's different from everywhere else in this neighborhood. And I like the things you tell me . . ."

"Stay!"

She takes a step forward and hugs him. As always, he remains motionless, unable to make the slightest movement. Ouardya senses this. Ever since she has known him she has never tried to push things too far.

"You know that if you stay, I shall drink less."

She takes Boualem's hand, squeezes it, and puts it on her breast. The only gesture she dares make. She closes her eyes, opens them again, and smiles at him.

"I forgot to bring you your glass of water."

11

BOUALEM DOES NOT REALLY REMEMBER HOW HE HEARD OF OUARDYA, this woman who is so very different, a piece of valuable wreckage washed up in the middle of Bab el-Oued. He knew she was intellectual. "She reads books, you see! Then again, she doesn't spend her time with the shrews who live on the terraces. Well, anyway, that's what they say . . ."

He also knew that she lived there, alone, in that apartment. The young men of the neighborhood talked about her, describing her in different terms according to their fantasies, since almost no one went to see her. The children were frankly afraid of her. "A witch who drinks the blood of those who fall into her hands!" At night, beneath the porches of the blocks of flats or in the courtyards, she was often the subject of conversation. "But what on earth is she doing here, for heaven's sake! Instead of living in the smart districts, in Hydra, for example!" "No one goes to see her. She's all alone. A total recluse." "Another madwoman! Algeria has more and more of them . . ." "What about money, where does she get the bread to live on? She has to eat, after all." "What a scandal! A single woman living on her own in an apartment, when there's a housing shortage and families living on top of one another . . ." "Who knows! Perhaps there's a commandant or a colonel protecting her . . ." "Have you ever seen a man in her flat?"

The first time Boualem met Ouardya it was like attraction followed by an irresistible urge. Uncontrollable. Identical to that which hurled him onto the terrace in a few seconds to tear down the loudspeaker disturbing his sleep. It all started with a strange discussion that intrigued him. A youngster from the neighborhood was leaving to do his military service. During the beery evening celebrating his departure he revealed in his drunken stupor that he had been doing the shopping for Ouardya for years. "Yes! She's called Ouardya . . . I swear on my mother's head, may she die this instant!" In an aside, to puff up his importance, he confided to Boualem that from time to time she allowed him to do some "nice, gentle things" to her, but that what he found amazing was that each week she had to have her supplies of wine! "Wine? You're kidding!" "I swear, on my mother's head, may she die this instant . . . ten bottles of wine a week . . . and I'm the one who's been buying them . . ." Then the conversation had turned to other things.

Time had passed and Boualem had forgotten what the youngster had told him. He was suddenly reminded of it one morning when coming home after a long night in the bakery, followed by a few hours in the hammam to get clean. He passed by Aami Abdallah, the wine merchant of the Basséta district, just as he was unloading a supply of crates of Mascara. Within a few minutes, without knowing why, Boualem had bought three bottles, climbed the five flights of stairs, knocked on the door, and found himself breathless, bashful but excited, the bottles in his hand, face-to-face with Ouardya who, once she had got over her surprise, smiled at him and invited him in.

12

Mess THE ÉMIGRÉ MAKES HIS WAY INTO THE MAIN HALL OF THE telephone exchange of Bab el-Oued. He slips into a telephone booth with no doors, takes from his jacket a roll of five dinar coins, agitatedly dials a number, and holds the phone to his ear. Anxiety gnaws at him. He redials several times because all the lines are busy. When, finally, he hears the phone ringing, he wipes the sweat from his forehead with his hand and starts speaking rapidly with his distinctive Parisian accent.

"Ma! Is that you? Yeah, yeah! Couldn't manage it before . . . Too difficult . . . Yeah, yeah . . . The heatwave. I've sneaked out of work to phone you. What about Krimo, what's he been doing? Yeah, I've been back to the embassy . . . but if you haven't got a passport, they don't want to know. I'm not getting anywhere, mother! It's driving me mad! You can't imagine."

Mess slips the coins in the payphone as needed. He is a small, odd-looking figure about five-foot-two, bursting out of his tight gray *qamis* over which he wears a scruffy black leather jacket; he doesn't seem to mind the heat. He bounces up and down while speaking. It's a habit he has, a sign of his agitation.

A dozen or so people have collected round the phone booth. In the suffocating heat, they impatiently wait their turn to use the phone while listening in to the conversation. Mess finally notices this. He gets annoyed. "What's the matter with you all? Can't you leave me alone? No, mother, I'm not speaking to you . . ."

Seeing Mess's threatening manner and tone of voice the eavesdroppers step back.

"You can't imagine! I can't take any more of this. I'm not getting anywhere. There isn't anywhere to get. Krimo'll have to sort it out. He'll have to go to the association. He's got all the info. And how about the kids, how are they? OK, got to go . . . Run out of change. Yes, yes, I'm eating OK. Yes, that's sorted out, I'm staying at a friend's house. Krimo'll just have to go to the association. We're going to be cut off. Big hug to you all. I'll call again when I can."

Mess hangs up. As always, talking to his mother upsets him. Leaving the phone booth, he glares at the next person.

"Up yours!"

The man, who hasn't understood the expression, gives him a smile.

Mess leaves the post office and goes out into the street, deep in thought.

It was in June 1986 that Mess's life started to fall apart. "Just my fucking luck! Down the metro, Bobigny station, early evening. Cops waiting at the exit. Routine identity check. A few packages of shit in my pockets to flog discreetly on my pitch. Quick trial, soon over. Fleury prison. Two years inside. I didn't know about the bugger of a double sentence though. I didn't know you got done twice over. Prison plus expulsion for immigrants . . . shoved straight on the next plane for Algiers."

What Mess really couldn't understand and accept was that he had been expelled though he was born in France and had a French passport. "It's getting me down, getting me down! I can't understand."

When he arrived at Algiers airport his passport was immediately confiscated by the Algerian police, anxious to collaborate with their French colleagues. "Makes you want to puke." He got two months in El Harrach prison, "a real palace, each day with its routine horrors. Worse than the jails they show you in American films." When he got out, Mess landed on the streets with only his bundle of clothes. Lost. Stuck. A stranger in his own country. He drifted for a few days in the dusty streets of the capital, then remembered he had some distant cousins in Kabylia. He turned up on their doorstep. But there, after a week of his company, his cousins let him know he was the kind of emigrant they could do without.

"Comes along empty-handed, lives off us, tells us some story about a passport and being expelled . . . With this heat scorching our lungs not to mention our own problems, well, we've got other worries—and he doesn't even speak Kabyle!"

Algiers once again. In the streets. Day follows day, dismal and with no prospects. "These fucking useless meetings . . ."

He was happier once he got to know others like himself. At the main telephone exchange a dozen or so young expelled emigrants, like him victims of the double sanction, adrift in the city, would get together to phone their parents in France when they had the money. It had become a habit. The place quickly became a meeting point. "We told each other the news from home, we were happy because the socialists had returned to power in France. They were going to abolish the law on double sentences. There was maybe even an association that was seriously going to take up our cases. A group of priests in Algiers was going to link up with them."

In the meantime the young exiles organized their lives as best they could in this openly hostile city where they were considered foreigners and treated as such. "In France they call me 'you wog,' here they call me 'you emigrant.' What's the difference?" A city where young people are not much liked anyway, especially if they are unlucky enough to be different. And as soon as these young exiles who have been forcibly sent back to Algeria open their mouths their difference becomes blatant.

After drifting under the arcades of the seafront and on wasteland at nightfall they finally discovered a shack on an abandoned building site, far from curious onlookers. In this flimsy hut they collected cardboard boxes to sleep in. Fortunately it was often hot. Mess was easily accepted. He was one of them. They told him of their day-to-day survival, with no job, continually harassed by the police, caught up in their problems of language and adaptation. And of their fear of nighttime, with its attendant dangers.

Timo, one of the young men forcibly repatriated from Lyons, told him that what they were all afraid of was "those fuckers who do the rounds at night looking for arses to screw." Usually their hunting ground was restricted to Port Saïd Square and Seafront Avenue where the homeless, adults and children, gathered. The "night rapists" drove up in their big cars and brutally pounced upon their victims. Sometimes they agreed to pay to enjoy the favors of the homeless kids. Mostly, however, you were lucky to get away at daybreak without having been beaten to death. Some of these pedophile maniacs, the most ruthless, were armed and didn't hesitate to use their guns.

Mess was unable to believe and accept these nightmarish stories. Algiers seemed rather quiet at night. The odd police patrol and not much nightlife. For years the majority of the population of Algiers had got used to going home at dusk. In the outlying districts the young men spent their evenings in front of the doors of the blocks of flats. But the city center seemed rather deserted.

One evening, the night rapists, or arse screwers as they were nicknamed in Algiers, discovered the émigrés' shack. About fifteen of them attacked without warning one night. A real raid. Mess was one of the few to escape. He came back next day and attempted a cautious recce of the place. All the others had disappeared. Only some traces of blood remained as proof of the previous night's violence. He spent a few more nights in the shack, hoping that his companions of misfortune would return, then, fearing for his safety, he decided to move on.

He started lurking around Bab el-Oued. "Here at least it was a really working-class neighborhood, and people were certainly more human." He helped unload vegetables at the market, sold birds, washed cars at the Climat de France stream, and began going regularly to the Hayat mosque to share the collective meals, the *ouaâdates,* during which the famous ritual couscous was distributed to the poor when there were funeral ceremonies or religious feasts. It was there he met Imam Rabah who allowed him to sleep in the mosque, in exchange for some cleaning.

Later on he heard, without being able to confirm it, a rumor that the young émigrés of the shack had been locked up in a villa before being moved to Oran and then sent down south. A major prostitution ring for both sexes, which had struck lucky that night. "There must be a God! Otherwise, where would I be now?" The mere thought of it brought Mess out in a cold sweat. "A rent-boy in Black Africa! Mother!"

Mess very quickly got on with Imam Rabah who quite naturally started teaching him the Koran. "What a drag!" because Mess was as allergic to the Arabic language as he was to hard work. He began pretending so as not to annoy the Imam, and especially so as not to lose out on the little perks of the mosque. He let his beard grow, just like everybody else. "It looks to me as if it will never grow normally!" He secretly hoped that sooner or later his passport problem would be settled and that he would be able to leave forever this city he hated.

BACK AT THE POST OFFICE, Mess, lost in his gloomy thoughts, crosses the main boulevard and narrowly avoids getting run over by a car. On the pavement he finds himself face-to-face with fat Mabrouk who calls out to him cheerfully, "Hi there, you emigrant!"

Mess frowns.

"Hi there, *smina.* I told you not to call me 'you emigrant'!"

Mabrouk pretends not to have heard.

"Beard growing well, is it?"

"Mind your own business, you heretic! Just you wait, I'll smash your Walkman one of these days!"

Mabrouk bursts out laughing.

"I'll believe that when I see it! There's a boat due any moment. I'll be getting some good stuff in."

"I'm not interested in your deals anymore."

Mabrouk takes him by the shoulder and pulls him along.

"I know you've changed. But anyway the meeting point is at Bab j'did. They say there'll be some English shirts. And some Tuborg lager."

Mess shakes off Mabrouk and acts offended.

"Piss off! You devil! Son of Satan!"

He strides rapidly away, as if he wanted to escape from temptation as quickly as possible. Mabrouk mockingly watches him leave. He is beginning to know Mess. He knows he will soon be along to have a look at his goods.

13

IN THE LIVING ROOM YAMINA IS TRYING ON A SLIP. HER MOTHER, LALLA Jamila, is bending over her, sewing it up, trying to avoid pricking her with the needle.

"You've grown up so quickly. I can hardly believe you are a woman now."

Yamina bows her head. For the last few months her mother has regularly been hinting at the idea of marriage. For Lalla Jamila the marriage of her sons and daughter will clearly be the crowning success of her life as a decent woman.

After her husband's death "with dignity, decently in his bed, far from those horrors to be found in dreadful hospitals," Lalla Jamila, despite her immense grief, did not fall into depression. She had neither the time nor the money for that. Her sewing machine was working full time and became the main source of income in the household. Fortunately she had nimble fingers and an astonishing capacity for work. She had no difficulty getting orders. She even spent some time in a workshop in the Casbah, which employed a dozen dressmakers. She stayed there for ten days but then gave up because the working conditions were abominable. "Hell on earth. Not even a window to get a breath of air. And then that smell of drains . . ."

Stability took the shape of a Mozabite wholesaler who specialized in children's clothing. Orders were regular and so was the money. The main thing was to work hard and to finish on schedule. Yamina had soon learned to sew and started helping her mother. She loved watching her work and hearing her five silver bracelets jangling as she sewed. She was lulled by the familiar humming of the sewing machine. During these quiet moments

Yamina could escape into her youthful fantasies. Sometimes a yelp from her mother made her jump. Whenever the needle pierced Lalla Jamila's finger Yamina felt the pain in herself. She would rush over to her mother, hug her affectionately, and kiss her tearfully.

Before falling in love, Yamina swore she would never leave her mother. And then things had started getting confused in her mind. Everything was becoming blurred. She dreamed of him, of being with him every second, every day, while at the same time clinging to her initial idea of remaining in this home with her mother forever and ever.

"A WOMAN? BIG DEAL! It makes no difference at all whether I'm a little girl or a woman! Always shut up inside here . . ."

"You know we mustn't annoy Saïd . . ."

"Mustn't annoy him! That's what I hear all day long! Because he's decided I mustn't go out to work I have to stay shut up in here."

"But you're not shut up. You know full well you can go out like any decent girl on Fridays to the mosque, and to the hammam, and to visit your cousins with me."

"But you don't realize that I really want and need to go out to work. And what's more, it would help us financially."

"What would really help us would be for you to make a fine match and produce some children for me. Okay, now I've finished, you can take it off."

Yamina takes off the slip, revealing her small white breasts. This is just the moment that Cherif, hiding behind a curtain in the living room, has been waiting for. His eyes are out on stalks. Seeing his sister's breasts disturbs him so much that he catches his feet in the curtains. Yamina hastily puts on a long garment. Once Lalla Jamila has got over her surprise, she goes for the child, raising her arm. She barely misses Cherif's head as he escapes at top speed.

"You little rascal! That's your latest trick, is it? Can you believe it, that little pervert peeking at his sister . . . And you could wear a bra, too, while we're at it."

Yamina smiles. She knows how often Cherif, her wicked little brother, has seen her breasts and the rest of her body. How could it be otherwise when they all live piled on top of one another, without any privacy whatsoever? And it is just the same or worse in all the families of the neighborhood where sometimes there may be fifteen people living in two rooms. Yamina does not know whether to be worried or to laugh when, at night, sleeping just a few centimeters away from their mother, she can hear Cherif moving about in the dark, fiddling with his little willy. What can she do about it?

"As soon as his pubic hairs start growing, he'll start sleeping in the kitchen, since 'Mr.' Saïd wants to have the second bedroom to himself."

That was what Lalla Jamila had decided.

14

SAÏD, FAR FROM SUCH TRIVIAL PURSUITS, IS EXTREMELY BUSY. FOR THE past few days he has been making extensive inquiries, having decided to pursue his investigations as far as possible. After the morning prayer his group of faithful militants charges down to Rocher Carré. They know that in that God-forsaken place you can run to ground all the riffraff of Bab el-Oued. If he only could, Rashid would like to "napalm off the face of the earth this den of tramps and degenerates."

Mess, however, hasn't the faintest idea what napalm could be. "One of those complicated whatnots, like the atom bomb. Like the insecticides you use against cockroaches." It gives Mess the creeps, but he knows from experience that there is no point in having a discussion with Rashid. The young immigrant with bandy legs thinks, "I hope to God he never gets his hands on napalm . . . He's bad enough as it is with his Kalashnikov!"

Saïd twists his ankle, which puts him in an even fouler mood.

"See what I mean, there's more empty wine bottles here than rocks."

Ali, Tahar, and Karim, the three junkies, are there as usual, sheltering among the rocks. Seeing the three leather-jacketed *qamis* approaching, Karim stops the cassette and, in a resigned voice, says to Tahar, "Hide the gear."

Ali looks up.

"I don't know how they can stand wearing their leather jackets in this heat!"

A few minutes later, Saïd, in a smarmy voice, gets straight to the point.

"You know, Ali, I've just got hold of a really good Syrian cassette. Some religious *medh*. I can pass it on to you if you like. It'll make a nice change from that noise you listen to!"

The three of them, who have smoked a great deal, listen with half an ear to what Saïd is telling them.

"Well, apart from the Moroccan cassettes, some *chaabi* and a bit of *rai*, nothing else gets past my eardrums . . . I have a block about it! Don't know why. Must be something wrong with me!" answers Ali sarcastically in his resigned voice.

Saïd gets nasty, takes a tougher line. "You moron! Trying to be clever! Remember we know exactly what you are up to all day long."

Tahar dares stand up to Saïd. "So what? Joined the cops, have you?"

"This neighborhood's going to be thoroughly cleaned up! And not by the cops either. By us! And I hope you've nothing to do with the disappearance of the loudspeaker."

"What loudspeaker?"

"The one that was stolen off the terrace of our block of flats. The loudspeaker broadcasting the word of God from the mosque."

The three of them look at one another, astonished. Ali bursts out laughing. "Well, what a laugh! I don't really see what anyone would do with a loudspeaker."

Tahar also has a laugh and adds, "We aren't intending to start a pop group!"

Saïd, annoyed, makes a face and says cuttingly, "That's right! Make me laugh! I bet you'd be capable of stealing to buy and sell your shitty dope. You think no one saw you looting the shop windows of Ben M'hidi Street, in October during the riots."

Tahar goes pale. "So you're accusing us, are you?"

"Oh, piss off! We're keeping an eye on you."

Saïd's companions approach threateningly. Rashid shouts at Karim, "You've got the message! Shove off!"

Ali, Tahar, and Karim do as they are told. They get up with difficulty and collect their belongings. Rashid goads them in his aggressive voice, "You'll join the faithful sooner or later. And you'll bow down low before the Almighty!"

The five militants shout out in unison, "Allah Akbar!"

Proud of himself, Saïd strokes his beard. "These three idiots are completely stoned."

Rashid watches them move away.

"Appalling! Nothing but zombies . . . I don't think they'd have been able to steal the loudspeaker."

Saïd shrugs his shoulders and looks towards the huge block of concrete. "Let's take a look over there! I can see another group."

15

L EANING AGAINST A WALL, BOUALEM IS WAITING QUIETLY. HE HAS TAKEN up a position about five hundred yards from the entrance to the famous *fartas* hammam, so called because of the dramatic misfortune which happened to a group of twenty women. Their hair fell out one afternoon as a result of using some infected soft soap made and sold by the owner of the establishment. After a few minor tussles with the law the said owner was sentenced to pay compensation to his victims, then it was back to business as usual.

Nothing much could be done against this man who had become rich after Independence thanks to his loyal support of the dignitaries in the régime. Now he owns ten hammams, a few hotels and bars, as well as other more or less legal establishments. Since the dramatic incident the proprietor had been nicknamed Yul Brynner and the hammam called *fartas*. They no longer sold homemade soft soap there but they still had a large number of clients: their water was never cut off.

Yamina and her mother appear through the raised flowered curtain. Both are wearing the *hidjab* and carrying bags containing their clothes and towels. Four children are with them: Cherif and three of their neighbors' children. Their faces are all pink and glowing after the steam in the hammam. Cherif's face is positively radiant since these sessions allow him to gawp his fill at the naked women. Boualem moves to one side so as not to be seen. He lets them get ahead of him, then begins to follow them up the road. After a few minutes he catches up with them, makes as if to overtake and recognize them.

"Hello, aunt El Hadja!* Did you enjoy the hammam?"

Lalla Jamila stops and smiles at him. He kisses her.

"Hello, Boualem! How are you? We haven't seen you for a long time. How's your family? Hanifa, Kader?"

"They're fine! Everyone's well, thank you."

He turns to Yamina and shyly holds out his hand to greet her.

"Hello, Yamina!"

While shaking Yamina's hand he discreetly slips her a folded note. Yamina masks her initial surprise and smiles broadly at Boualem while concealing the note.

Hadja is the correct form of address to a woman who has been on the pilgrimage to Mecca [translator's note].

"Hello, Boualem!"

Jokingly Boualem says, "I was afraid you wouldn't shake my hand now you're wearing the *hidjab*."

Yamina coyly lowers her gaze. Her mother gives her a sidelong glance and laughs.

"Well! We've known you so long! Yamina wears the *hidjab* to protect herself, not just to look right like all the other pretend Muslim women in the district."

Yamina adjusts her scarf and gazes at Boualem. "I can also decide not to touch a man's hand if I want."

Boualem moves away from the two women. "Well, OK, I'll be off then. Bye!"

Hands in his pockets, he continues on his way. Lalla Jamila watches him disappear.

"He's a nice boy. And a hard worker. You could be a bit nicer to him."

"As my brother Saïd says, in our neighborhood it isn't done to be nice to young men."

"Yes, but that doesn't apply to Boualem. You've known him since you were children."

Yamina blushes.

"I feel thirsty after the hammam. I could do with a lemonade."

16

A T THE FLOWER OF BAB EL-OUED TUESDAY NIGHTS ARE PARTICULARLY busy for no apparent reason. On Wednesdays, bread consumption soars. Hassan-the-baker has never understood why. "A funny day! Heaven alone knows why!" Five ovenloads need to be prepared and the youngsters of the morning shift will be producing another three. "Fortunately there's no shortage of flour at the moment." Boualem and Mabrouk are shoveling loaves in and out of the oven at an incredible rate. Hassan is humming as he prepares the croissants. Mabrouk whispers to Boualem, "Have you heard about the loudspeaker?"

Boualem looks up quickly and stares at Mabrouk. "What loudspeaker?"

"The one from the mosque, that someone stole from your terrace."

Boualem shrugs his shoulders and pretends to be surprised.

"I was thinking it didn't seem as loud as before."

Mabrouk hesitates before continuing, "They're making an awful fuss about it in the neighborhood. I'm sure it's been sold by now. Very popular for weddings."

"Really?" says Boualem, casually.

"Yes! Unless it was the cops who did it. The infidels! May God protect us."

Mabrouk sticks on his Walkman earphones. His sudden religious outbursts make Boualem smile. The fat cook takes off his chef's hat and observes Boualem with the careful scrutiny of someone you can't fool.

"I saw Saïd, Rashid, and 'the beards.' They're not happy. They're questioning everyone, they're prowling round everywhere. You'd think they were Kojak and his detectives."

Boualem smiles and jokes, "I can quite see Saïd walking around with a lollipop stick . . ."

Mabrouk doesn't seem to appreciate the joke and looks his mate up and down.

"I hope you've nothing to do with it!"

Boualem doesn't flinch.

"Why do you ask me that?"

"Because from what I can make out there's going to be trouble. They want to teach everyone a lesson. And I can understand them. Just think of it, fancy stealing a loudspeaker belonging to the mosque! That's an unforgivable sin!"

"Yes, for sure . . ."

Mabrouk does not notice Boualem's sarcastic tone.

"An unforgivable sin."

He rubs his nose.

"Saïd doesn't like you very much, does he?"

"So it would seem!"

Mabrouk makes a gesture alluding to the beards.

"If you were one of them, you'd be their leader."

Boualem shakes his head sadly.

"I don't want to be the leader of anything at all. I say my prayers, that's enough."

Mabrouk gives him a friendly warning: "Anyway, watch out!"

Boualem takes offense.

"Watch out? What does that mean? What are you accusing me of?"

"No, but you never know. I know you . . ."

Mabrouk puts the earphones back on to signal the end of the discussion. But he takes them off again immediately. "Yes, I know you. And right now, in this neighborhood, I can smell trouble."

Getting no response, Mabrouk shrugs his shoulders and puts his earphones back on. He takes them off once again.

"D'you think the other one, there, that Rashid-Peshawar . . . D'you think he really went to Afghanistan?"

"How should I know?"

Boualem pushes the wooden shovel right to the back of the oven.

"God alone knows!"

17

FOUR HOURS LATER BOUALEM AND MABROUK FINALLY LEAVE THE bakery, exhausted. They walk down a narrow deserted street just as the sun is rising. The contents of torn rubbish bags litter the pavements. A few cats are fighting to snatch the refuse lying around the street. Two kids pass by in silence, carrying a crate of sardines. The two bakers walk up to a parked car. Gray curtains are drawn across all the windows, including the windscreen and rear window. Mabrouk taps on the window. The curtain twitches aside. A young man, his eyes heavy with sleep, smiles sadly at them. Mabrouk holds up a paper bag.

"Hi Omar! Here's some hot croissants!"

Omar opens the window and swiftly grabs the bag.

"Hello Mabrouk! Hi, Boualem! Thanks!"

Mabrouk smiles.

"Any nice dreams? A Mercedes? A BMW perhaps?"

Omar smiles sadly.

"I didn't dream at all."

Boualem sees a shape covered by a sheet stretched out on the back seat. Mabrouk has also noticed it.

"Is Hamid sleeping here too?"

Omar stretches and yawns.

"Yes! He's had a row with his wife because she's announced she's pregnant."

"Again?"

Omar shrugs and takes a croissant out of the bag.

"Have a nice day!"

He winds up the window and draws the curtain across it as Mabrouk and Boualem walk away in silence. A few yards further on Mabrouk comments in his hoarse voice after the sleepless night, "It's lucky he has a car to sleep in."

"Is it true there are sixteen of them in a two-room flat?"

Mabrouk shrugs and says casually: "No! There's eighteen of them."

"What a life!"

"And what's more, Omar has just got married, the fool. His wife is still living with her parents. He goes to see her once a week. And there's the other one, Hamid's wife, who's going to drop yet another kid . . . Their fifth."

THE TWO FRIENDS are both leaning on the old counter in the little café on the corner of the main street of Bab el-Oued, the only place open at five in the morning. They are the only clients; despite being exhausted, neither of the two wants to go home to sleep. It comes from working at night. When extremely tired, they prefer to drink three or four coffees before falling into a heavy sleep lasting into the early afternoon. Fatah, the humpbacked old man who works in the coffee bar, is still half-asleep as he fiddles with the coffee machine.

Mabrouk takes out three croissants from a second paper bag he has brought with him from the bakery and starts eating.

"The flour is dreadful at the moment . . ."

Boualem lights a cigarette.

"Come on, Fatah! Get on with it! Let's have a *goudroun* and a *half-half* in a glass."

"Wait till the machine heats up!"

Mabrouk stretches.

"Shit! I ache all over. Especially my back . . ."

"Thank God we're off tonight."

Mabrouk suddenly stares at Boualem.

"You're the one who pinched the loudspeaker from the terrace!"

Boualem smiles and answers without looking at Mabrouk, "Yes, I am!"

Mabrouk whistles in amazement.

"Wow! That's incredible! What got into you?"

Boualem drags on his cigarette.

"If only I knew! My God! It was when I slung it into the sea that I realized the mess I'd got myself into."

Mabrouk nervously cracks his fingers.

"And do you think it was a sin?"

Irritated, Boualem watches the man getting the coffee machine going.

"Oh, leave me alone."

Mabrouk bolts down a second croissant.

"Perhaps we could try to fish it out. Whereabouts did you throw it?"

"Off Rocher Carré. And now I don't want to talk about it anymore."

Mabrouk pretends to get angry.

"Well, I'm talking about it because with a thing like this Saïd'll have the whole neighborhood behind him. And you'll see, he'll finish you off. We were doing fine, everyone with their own little racket, and now you've messed it all up."

"You're dreaming! Things'll never ever be the same in Bab el-Oued. Ever. I'm telling you. And not because of the bloody loud-speaker either. Now lay off me."

Suddenly Boualem can hear nothing but a deafening noise in his ears, something powerful, heavy, unpleasant—an invisible but almost palpable mass grabbing him by the throat, creeping into his flesh and bones, filling his head and brain before spreading through his entire body. A thundering inside him louder than the kneading machine at work. He has learned from experience that he has to get to sleep soon to prevent an explosion. Three or four times already this strange thing has overwhelmed him and each time he thought his last hour had come. Without another word he leaves the café and a startled Mabrouk behind.

18

SAÏD HAS DRAWN A BLANK ALL WEEK WITH HIS INITIAL INVESTIGATIONS and has also failed in his attempts to recover the loudspeaker and punish the wrongdoer. He has now organized a meeting of his group in a cellar graciously provided by a fellow beard. They intend this place to become the future headquarters of the party now being formed.

The youngest of the militants, Tewfik, crouching near the *meïda,* the folds of his *qamis* held between his thighs, is gracefully filling the little tea glasses in Moroccan style. The other members of the group, a dozen or so, sitting cross-legged on mats, serious and extremely tense, surround Saïd who is chairing the meeting. In his usual edgy way he speaks loudly and quickly, analyzing the situation in the neighborhood, indicating the work still remaining to be done to win over the young, and especially—the main point of the meeting—he is attempting to persuade his friends of the need to find the loudspeaker and the thief.

"If the police had done it, we would know. And I don't see why they would. It must be someone who did it deliberately to annoy us, to test our strength. Someone from the neighborhood. "

Tewfik stops pouring and says, "We could start collecting money to buy another one."

Saïd screams, "No! That's not the point. This neighborhood is ours and we can't let this pass."

The young Tewfik does not give up. "Look, Saïd, I think we've got more important things to do. We've got to organize the summer camps for the children of Climat de France."

Saïd, annoyed, gives him a withering glance. He yells, "That will get done, for heaven's sakes! The camps will be organized and the children will get to the seaside. But we're meeting now to prepare our strategy and reestablish our authority. And I'm telling you, this loudspeaker business must be settled."

Rashid seizes the opportunity to go further and, while he's at it, to brag a little. "I agree! It's urgent. I know some people are starting to find it a joke. It might put ideas into people's heads."

"Let's give ourselves a week . . ."

19

AT ROCHER CARRÉ THE WAVES ARE SMASHING INTO THE ROCKS AS usual and battering the large concrete blocks. Suddenly Mabrouk's head emerges. He shakes himself and takes a deep breath. Boualem appears a few seconds later. He too fills his lungs.

Three days after their discussion in the café, Mabrouk came looking for Boualem at his house and persuaded him to go along to the place where the loudspeaker had been thrown into the sea. Mabrouk is taking this matter very seriously. He does not want Boualem to get into trouble, and as he has told him very bluntly, he is in favor of maintaining good relations in the neighborhood. Back to the status quo, which would suit everyone. For the last few months Mabrouk had been noticing the radical changes in people's attitudes. He was worried by the crowds of believers assembling each Friday, coming in from the outlying districts, swarming into the mosques of Bab el-Oued. He could sense the growing tension, display of intolerance, and the unhealthy atmosphere that boded ill. Bab el-Oued was visibly changing and he didn't like it at all. They needed to find that bloody loudspeaker, quietly replace it on the terrace, and just forget about the whole thing.

For the last two hours they have been diving nonstop but have found nothing.

"We're wasting our time! The undertow must have swept it away ages ago."

Mabrouk coughs. "My lungs hurt."

Boualem climbs up onto the rocks. "Oh, let's forget it."

"And the water's freezing too!"

"It was your big idea. The loudspeaker must be in Spain or Marseilles by now. Or perhaps it's made it to America."

Mabrouk, large and awkward, is struggling to cling to the rocks. The waves are starting to buffet him. He grazes himself on a sharp edge. "Shit, it'll be a sea urchin next!"

Boualem retraces his steps and hauls him up. "It stinks around here. We might get some disease."

Mabrouk shakes his heavy body and says, sarcastically, "Couldn't you've slung it into a beer barrel? It'd have been a lot more fun diving in."

Boualem doesn't smile at the joke. He takes a comb from his jacket and carefully does his hair. Mabrouk rummages in a Marlboro bag and takes out a towel. He rubs his back, then his ears.

"What was up with you the other day at the café? You looked like death warmed over!"

"If only I knew! It's some kind of noise. It gets into my head and drives me mad. It feels like it's eating up my brain. I don't know."

"Go and see a doctor, mate. Maybe you're going a bit funny. It's quite mad . . . stealing a loudspeaker and throwing it in the sea, that's a crazy thing to do! Now if you'd robbed a bank . . ."

Mabrouk watches the waves breaking on the rocks. His eyes sting with the salt. He closes them and drifts off.

20

WHEN CHUBBY MABROUK STARTED WORKING IN THE BAKERY, HE HAD just made a firm, irrevocable decision: he would never cross the sea again. He would never take the plane again because on his last Paris-Algiers trip the Air Algeria Boeing had very nearly crashed. At least, that's what he had imagined when, high above the Mediterranean, he had heard suspicious noises and felt strange vibrations. When he saw the expression of the air hostess who was clutching her seat for dear life, that was it. That was the last straw. He would never forget that terrible trip.

Yet he had certainly been back and forth ever since he was old enough to have a passport. Just like hundreds of others from the poor neighborhoods of Algiers he found himself in a comfy little racket smuggling clothes, which involved transporting large bags directly from the sweatshops of the Sentier district in Paris. With the protection of one of the smugglers he had no difficulty in getting his first passport. He was able to become a smuggler— a *trabendist.*

Trabendo was the slang term invented by the young people to describe the contraband after it developed from being a flourishing practice during the 1970s into a full-blown national phenomenon. A black market economy had taken root in Algeria, making up for the stagnation of the official economy, undermined by bureaucracy, corruption, and endemic embezzlement. *Trabendo* was also the result of the wheeler-dealing of the so-called political thinkers following one another as heads of government and whose major concern was getting rich quick on income from oil, under the cover of nationalist and socialist slogans.

Mabrouk was not interested in all this rubbish. What mattered to him was that the work should be simple, good fun, and well paid. "Better than being a doctor or engineer." The system worked perfectly. There was an extensive, long-standing, and well-organized network. The professionalism of the mysterious bosses in charge of the smuggling made it all a lot easier. "A real pleasure! Better than lounging around or selling cigarettes in the scorching sun."

The boss gave him a ticket with a reservation for the return journey, a bonus of two hundred francs and a two-day stopover in Paris. As soon as he got there he knew what to do and where to go. There was no time to be lost. Usually there were five or six "suitcase carriers" travelling together. Once they had settled into the Goutte d'Or hotel run by "Uncle Kassim" they waited for the local middleman who brought them the clothes and their evening meal, usually a huge sizzling-hot pizza.

After that, work could begin. They had to remove all the inessential labels, hangers, etc. This was crucial since the bags could then be stuffed full of clothes and all surplus weight eliminated. These rather monotonous tasks could take up most of the night, but as they were all mates together they had a good laugh telling one another dirty stories. "Having a ball."

Next morning they were allowed off the leash for a couple of hours to "have a look round" (Mabrouk was happy enough just walking up and down the boulevard St. Denis a few times ogling the prostitutes) or to spend their pocket money. Their two hundred francs could be used to purchase little things like cheese, whisky, cigarettes, chocolate, gadgets, which they resold at the fluctuating *trabendo* rate of Algiers. "Profit all round! Thanks be to the Lord." Those were the good old days. Chubby Mabrouk always looked back on that time with a touch of nostalgia. Paris, Marseilles, Rome, Barcelona, sometimes pushing as far as Istanbul or Damascus. That was a time when Mabrouk enjoyed life and met fun people.

But at the moment Mabrouk, who felt he was getting on, was taking it easy in the bakery. Far from the growing problems and risks due to an increasingly complex situation and the *trabendo* bosses who were waging a pitched battle to dominate the market. Mabrouk also knew that other forms of *trabendo* existed and were flourishing, such as using large trucks supposedly crossing Algeria from Morocco. They were stuffed full of goods which "fell off the back of a lorry" during the trip and were controlled by people who were untouchable. "There's where things really get scary."

Mabrouk felt at home in the bakery in the company of the taciturn Boualem whom he liked and respected and Hassan, their jovial boss, who managed to create a relaxed atmosphere despite his sometimes irritating jokes. Mabrouk discovered he had in fact achieved a certain maturity: he felt he was becoming rather bourgeois.

AT THE AGE OF TWELVE Mabrouk, the youngest in a family of twelve children, was thrown out of school for disruptive behavior and had found his first little job in his neighborhood: washing cars by the stream making its way down the steep slope from the district of the Climat de France, behind the huge tower blocks. A little stream whose source was unknown. It appeared in the region of Ben Aknoun and quietly flowed down the hills to the sea. A real gift for car owners when there was a water shortage in the capital. Mabrouk and his pals didn't like this at all. "They're coming to use this water free of charge! It's not fair; the stream runs through our neighborhood—you could even say it's our stream!" After a period of observation the teenagers set up a gang and decided to make life difficult for the tight-fisted car owners so as to resume control of the water and exploit it themselves. They began stealing everything from inside the cars. Or they even peed straight into the water making sure they were seen by the car owners filling their jerrycans. The drivers finally gave in, knowing when they were beaten. The kids then "nationalized" the stream. They immediately fixed the rates: a carwash cost between thirty and forty dinars, including soap and polishing.

The stream offered another opportunity to the kids. It had a highly strategic position, since the ancient goods trucks using this route took an inordinately long time to climb the hill. In between carwashes, the kids took advantage of this to jump on the back of the trucks and pinch sacks of semolina, crates of lemonade, or anything which came to hand, shocking their cardriver-clients by their brazen behavior. But their racket didn't last long. It came to an end when a brute of a bastard just out of prison appeared on the scene and, since he was older and tougher, decided arbitrarily that from now on he would be in charge of the carwashes. Sickened by this, Mabrouk gave up and started tramping the streets for a few years, down in the doldrums, before becoming a *trabendist.*

21

THE ROAD SNAKING DOWN THROUGH THE ROUGH VEGETATION ON the hillside of Sidi Bennour connects the district of Notre Dame d'Afrique with that of Bouzaréah, in the north of Algiers. There is not much traffic there because of the many bends and countless potholes. Yet at the top you have a magnificent view of the basilica, the stadium, the Jewish and Christian cemeteries adjoining one another in Bologhine, of Bab el-Oued, of the Admiralty, and above all of the limitless sea, stretching away into the distance. A splendid picture, a feeling of peace. Saïd is standing alone at the roadside, rather out of place in this deserted area, absentmindedly fiddling with his beard and looking vaguely down at his neighborhood at the bottom of the hill. The sound of the nearby cicadas barely drowns out the usual muffled noise of cars and people coming from below.

A large, shiny, midnight-blue BMW silently appears from round a bend. It slows down and glides to where Saïd is standing. The squeal of brakes makes him start with surprise and turn his head. He shows no reaction except for a slight grimace, which he immediately suppresses. He saunters toward the vehicle, the soles of his Adidas crunching loudly on the gravel.

There are two people sitting inside the BMW. The driver is a young fair-haired man with a mustache, distinguished-looking, whose eyes are hidden behind large sunglasses. When he lights a cigarette his solid gold signet ring glitters. Aware of the effect he is producing, he seems to enjoy flaunting his ring when it catches Saïd's glance. The passenger, concealed by the nearly closed tinted window, addresses Saïd in a gravelly authoritarian voice, that of an older man, rather sure of himself, hammering home his words to make sure he is understood.

"You've been rather hard to get hold of recently . . ."

Saïd does not answer. Being deliberately provocative, he leans casually against the door and puts his hand on the gleaming blue metal. He is delighted to notice his greasy fingers leaving prints on the paintwork.

"It wouldn't do to forget us, otherwise . . ."

Saïd interrupts. He blusters, on edge, "OK, OK! What d'you want?"

Saïd's tone doesn't seem to bother the man.

"Us? Nothing . . . You know we never want anything. Just to see you now and again as agreed. You haven't forgotten?" The fair-haired man with the signet ring reveals his perfect teeth in a vague smile. Saïd is fuming with impatience. Once again he places his large hand on the car. The fair-haired man has noticed his nails are nearly scratching the paintwork. He frowns with annoyance, opens his mouth to say something, then changes his mind. Saïd leans forward slightly to look more closely at the man's face.

"Well, I don't like these meetings."

"It's not a matter of liking them. What matters is that when we come looking for you . . ."

Saïd surveys the deserted road as if he were afraid of being seen in the company of these strange people. Edgy and tense, he once again doesn't allow the man to finish his sentence. "OK. Now you have found me. "

"Yes, we've found you and that's enough for the moment. There'll be something new soon. We'll let you know . . ."

The fair-haired man with the signet ring indicates that the interview is over by starting up the car. The motor purrs into life and the BMW takes off. A few meters further on it stops suddenly and reverses to where Saïd is still standing. The elderly man leans out and points at Saïd's face.

"By the way, Saïd, you've put too much kohl on your left eye."

The noise of the roaring motor mingles with the mocking laughter of the man with the signet ring as the car surges forward.

The midnight-blue BMW disappears. The sound of the cicadas fills the air once again. Motionless, Saïd seems fixed to the spot, rigid with hatred, anger churning up his guts. His face has turned into a waxen mask.

The ambiguous relationship he has with these two mysterious, cynical individuals began during the heady days of the riots of October 1988. The whole thing began one night, in a brothel. He still doesn't know how it will end. A mistake, a night he would regret all his life. But he feels in some confused way that it won't turn out well; he also knows there's nothing he can do, it is entirely out of his hands.

22

AT THE SAME TIME ELSEWHERE, ON THE IMMENSE STONE SQUARE IN front of the basilica of Notre Dame d'Afrique, just a few hundred meters below as the crow flies, Rashid has collected around him a group of a dozen or so schoolchildren who are listening agog to him telling of his exploits as a veteran of the war with Afghanistan.

"There weren't that many of us, can't have been more than six, when the Russians arrived. They surrounded us with their tanks, rocket-launchers, and all their heavy equipment. They were the élite troops. I had my 'Kalash' with me. I thought, I've had it, it's curtains for me. Well you aren't going to believe this, but when the communists started to gun us down, a miracle occurred, through God's will. Their bullets swerved off course. None came our way. We were protected by a kind of magnetic field. Through God's grace. The communists couldn't touch us."

The schoolchildren are listening to Rashid with respect and great attention. Boualem emerges from the funicular connecting Bologhine and Notre Dame d'Afrique. He crosses the square rapidly and disappears into the church. He does not notice Rashid, surrounded by the group of young people. Rashid, though, has seen Boualem and is intrigued by his unexpected appearance in this place.

"If you have any questions, feel free to ask."

One of the schoolchildren grabs hold of him.

"Tell us about the plane you shot down with your Kalashnikovs."

Rashid has all these stories down pat. He believes them even if they didn't exactly happen to him. But they might have.

When, at the age of eighteen, just barely emerging from adolescence, he got on to the Brussels-London-Karachi circuit, he was passionately in favor of this war of liberation that the "Afghan moujaheddin brothers" were waging against the Russian communist invaders occupying their country. Algeria bored him deeply; he was fed up each day. He was disgusted by the *hogra* on every street corner, and then again the stories of the fighters' exploits were so exciting. These modern sagas were told in the "liberal" mosques, in the fundamentalist campsites, in the sports halls, and at any and every opportunity. It was said that the young Algerian volunteers were always in the front line. They were the bravest, the most intrepid, of course. From time to time it was learned, alas, that a few coffins were returning or that certain people had sacrificed themselves and died as martyrs to Islam. Discretion was the rule. The young men were given a hero's burial.

When his turn came, Rashid left, happy as never before. He said his good-byes to his parents and asked them to forgive him for all the bad things he had done in the past, convinced he would perish in that far-off country and never see them again. The trip was long and the difficulties manifold, but at the end was the supreme and sacred action: the *jihad*. On arrival reality was less romantic. He found himself in Peshawar, on the frontier with Pakistan, and he was given the exalted task of organizing sanitary arrangements in a refugee camp, which actually meant cleaning the camp with the other foreign volunteers. At first he found this normal and necessary but he was chafing with impatience to go and fight. He was taken on a few marches, in the course of which he actually touched the wonderful Kalashnikov he had been dreaming of. But as for crossing into Afghanistan and fighting, nothing doing.

He started getting bored and began missing Algeria. He couldn't understand why he was not allowed to fight despite being in good physical health. After two years he was demobilized; the Afghan political leader thanked him and advised him to return home. "Algeria is being throttled by the *taghouts* and will soon need your services and your faith!"

Rashid returned somewhat sheepishly, not having been able to put into practice his bravery as a warrior. Yet his head was stuffed full of all the stories circulating in the *maquis*. In the bottom of his rucksack was his fighter's uniform, tangible proof of his time spent there and of his service record. That was better than nothing. At Bab el-Oued he was quickly respected and feared; nicknamed Peshawar, of course! He never took off his brown beret after that. He soon joined Saïd's group since Saïd's rabble-rousing suited him perfectly. In his heart of hearts he hoped that one fine day a Kalashnikov would fall into his hands once again. "The day is nigh! Then I shan't need to travel hundreds of kilometers for the *jihad!*" Other young Algerians who, like Rashid, had left for Afghanistan were beginning to return home. Most of them really had participated in the guerrilla actions. They would soon become notorious. The Algeria of corruption, embezzlement, and hypocrisy had just spawned a new generation of young people imbued with intolerance and violence. Ready to sow death . . .

RASHID-PESHAWAR HAD NO TIME to tell another tall tale to the schoolchildren. He absolutely had to know what that miserable little Boualem could be up to in the church. Boualem, unaware of Rashid's presence near the church, calmly walks across the deserted space, his steps resounding on the stone floor. He stops, looks around him. In one of the front pews he recognizes Yamina, sitting alone. Boualem hastens toward her. The girl raises her head and gazes at him. She smiles. She is wearing her gray *hidjab* and a white headscarf. Boualem sits down beside her. He whispers, "Hello!"

Yamina gives him a friendly smile. "Hello! What a place to meet!"

Boualem smiles. "Just an idea. And at least we won't run into the wrong people."

"It reminds me of when I was a kid. You remember?"

"Yes!"

"When my mother used to bring us here to light candles."

"That was a bit strange though. A Muslim girl, lighting candles in a church . . ."

"They used to say that Madame d'Afrique, the Black Madonna, produced miracles."

Yamina points to the statue of the Black Madonna above the altar. "You see! She's still there, she hasn't changed." Boualem looks at the statue.

"My mother tried everything at the time. Sidi Yahia, Sidi Brahim, she even went to see the marabout of Tamanrasset."

"And that didn't help cure your father."

Yamina doesn't answer. She blinks and swallows before answering breathlessly, "I'm frightened!"

Boualem looks at her. "Why?"

"Because of what you've done. Whatever got into you?"

Boualem bursts out impulsively, as if to convince her, "I don't know. I can't explain. It woke me up. Sometimes I feel as if I'm going mad, with this kind of machine boiling inside my head."

Yamina leans close enough to touch him. "Stop talking nonsense. You've got to get hold of the loudspeaker and put it back."

Boualem smiles at her. He thinks of Yamina diving with him into the polluted water at Rocher Carré to look for the loudspeaker.

"I can't! I threw it into the sea."

"My God! You're crazy. And why did you want to see me?"

He moves close to Yamina. He hesitates, then teases her, "Um, to find out whether you were going to inform on me."

Yamina notices Boualem's smile.

"That's the only reason? Just to see if I was going to turn you in?"

"No! I wanted . . . I really wanted to see you. It's been such a long time."

Yamina is pensive.

"Well, I see you nearly every morning when you come back from the bakery half asleep."

Boualem wriggles on his bench.

"You had promised me . . ."

"We were children then. It's not the same now."

"Let me see your hair."

Yamina looks at him in surprise.

"My hair? Why?"

Boualem pretends to be annoyed.

"You've always got to have some reason. You don't understand that there are some things you just want, without being able to explain. Why, for example here and now, I want to see your hair."

Yamina, for the first time, looks deep into Boualem's eyes. Her modesty prevents her from letting go and openly expressing her love. When, a few days earlier, she read the message Boualem had slipped her as she left the hammam, she felt a strange shiver of excitement. Yet it was only about a meeting. She folded and unfolded the piece of paper, read and reread all day long the few scribbled words, crumpling up the paper until the text was illegible.

As of that sweet moment she lived only for their meeting. She loves Boualem. Has since she was a little girl. A feeling which appeared naturally, without her really knowing how. The chance outcome of friendship as children, of playing together on the stairway of the block of flats. Gradual transformation of friendship into love in the fullness of time. By now she knows that he is the only man she would wish to live with. Only him. It was so long since she had been this close to him! Alone in this immense space. So close as to be able to touch him. To kiss him.

And now, though he is there, close to her, and she close to him, they do not touch nor confess their passionate love for one another. They allow themselves to get bogged down in misunderstandings and unspoken words. She looks at him and silently begs him to understand her. He too looks at her, and his eyes are shining with love and desire. Yamina agrees to do what he has asked. Slowly she undoes her scarf and lets her long black hair loose. She giggles to conceal her feelings. "There you are! Happy now?"

Boualem admires Yamina's face and hair. He makes as if to touch her, then drops his hand without daring to.

"Thank you. Yes! You know, Yamina, I'm working hard to save a little money. And I'm beginning to think of the future. Even if it won't be easy . . ."

His words come out with difficulty. Boualem is silent. Yamina, preoccupied, stares smiling into space. Curbing her emotion, she quickly pulls herself together. Her face tightens.

"Do you still go to visit that weird woman who never goes out?"

"Yes! But that's different. She's unhappy and everyone rejects her."

"Everyone rejects her. But they say you're very good to her."

"Let's not talk about that."

Rashid, hiding behind a column, has been watching Boualem and Yamina for some time. He holds his breath so as to catch a few snatches of the conversation which the echo sends his way. He has heard what the two young lovers have said about the loudspeaker. A gloating feeling of satisfaction is growing inside him. He is already looking forward to seeing Boualem crushed like an insect, after he has informed Saïd of what he has seen and heard. "It was God's will that I was there!" Rashid wants to believe he has just penetrated to the heart of a monstrous conspiracy.

"Yes . . . It was God's will that I was there! Otherwise how can you explain the discovery of this wickedness! This sacrilege! My God! Saïd's sister!" The idea that Yamina is in this place, in this company, is unbearable to him. Yet he can't prevent the perverse tingle of pleasure coursing through his body, gradually neutralizing his hatred. He desperately wants more action. The idea which has been going round in his head for a few seconds is gradually taking shape. He is convinced that it is not Boualem sitting a few meters away on a bench, but he himself, Rashid, facing Yamina, and that it is for him that she has removed her scarf. For him, the friend, the faithful companion of Saïd, a good Muslim, a soldier of God. He who, until this blessed day, has never ever seen Yamina's hair nor this sparkling gaze, her eyes so big, so beautiful, her pupils so dilated with desire.

Rashid is aware of his shirt soaked with sweat sticking to his armpits. He would like to hear everything. Every little sentence. Every little word pronounced by Yamina. The slightest sigh. She is looking at Boualem, but that's only an illusion. She's really talking to him, Rashid, the hero of Peshawar. He's the one she wants. "What's keeping the faggot from screwing her now on the spot! What's he waiting for since he'll be massacred anyway?" Rashid's fingers splay out on the marble column; the purple veins pulsing through his temples swell to bursting point. "Get on with it, Rashid! Screw her! Screw her, Rashid! She's right next to you. For months you've only seen her when she goes into the mosque. Just a few seconds before she goes into the room set aside for women! You love those moments! You want her so much you use your organizer's position to give orders and gesticulate in the service to draw attention to yourself because you want her to notice you, to smile at you, to be affected by your presence. But she doesn't even see you. She's proud. Stuck up. Whereas here, at this moment, in a church, amongst the infidels, she is showing you her hair, she is smiling at you. She is smiling at you, Rashid. Look, she's going to take off her *hidjab.* For you! She's going to offer you the dampness of her body! You're going to penetrate her at the feet of the Black Madonna . . ."

Suddenly Rashid hears footsteps behind him. His fantasy is brutally shattered. He stops breathing. He flattens himself against the column so as not to be seen. His fingers press into the marble. He breaks his thumbnail. He recites a quick prayer to dispel the wicked thoughts that have just assailed him. "Allah will forgive me! Allah will forgive me!" Yamina and Boualem have also heard the footsteps. The young woman swiftly replaces her headscarf.

"I must go! It was crazy to have met here."

"I love you . . . Do you understand that?"

"I'm going to leave! Don't come out just yet."

She gets up hastily just as two people enter the church. A man aged about forty wearing a beige suit and a yellow shirt, with a reddish face, with smiling mischievous eyes, is accompanying an elderly woman wearing a light coat and walking with difficulty. Sunglasses conceal her blind eyes. In one hand she is clutching a rosary and in the other a white cane. She is guided by the man who is holding her arm. They stop close to the font and make the sign of the cross. Yamina slips past them and leaves the church.

The man admires the stained glass windows and the ex-voto offerings inside the basilica. He whispers a few words in the old lady's ear, then takes her by the shoulder and helps her forward. They sit down on a pew, in front of Boualem who has not moved, still affected by the moments he has spent in Yamina's company. Paulo speaks in a low voice but his words echo around. "If you could only see it, Auntie! How beautiful it still is! It hasn't changed. Not a bit. It feels as if I was here only yesterday."

The old woman nods.

"Yes. But it would have been better if we had bought candles. I had promised ten but now . . ."

Paulo is looking at Boualem who still has not moved and seems prostrate.

"I can't help that! The shop is shut. Perhaps they're not allowed to sell candles anymore. Or maybe they're on strike. I don't know. There isn't even a priest. How should I know? It's true, there's no priest."

He speaks to Boualem who is just standing up.

"Excuse me, young man! That shop outside, where they sell candles . . . do you happen to know why it's shut?"

Boualem answers in broken French, "No! I'm only here by . . . by chance . . ."

To avoid further questions, he hastens to the door. Rashid hides. He is pleased with what he has seen. He hasn't wasted his time, far from it. Now he can set in motion the machinery to crush Boualem.

Paulo admires the walls of the basilica.

"Great, Auntie! I shall describe the basilica to you. And afterwards I'll read you some of the ex-voto offerings. D'you realize, there's even an American astronaut who has visited the basilica!"

The aunt sighs and nods.

"Quite right too! It's the biggest in the world."

Paulo smiles indulgently.

"Well, maybe not quite! Never mind, shall I read them out to you now?"

23

BOUALEM, STILL PERTURBED BY HIS ENCOUNTER WITH YAMINA THE previous day, has agreed to go fishing from the rocks with his brother Kader. Kader carefully baits the lines. He knows exactly what to do to make sure the bait doesn't fall off the hook. The eels love it. He throws in a little *bromitch,* and sets up his three rods. Boualem, though, does not feel at all like fishing. Sitting on a rock, he smokes a cigarette and distractedly watches a steamer maneuvering to get out of the port. Kader wipes his hands as he too looks across at the ship.

"It's the *Tassili.* Tomorrow evening they'll be in Marseilles. Lucky things!"

Boualem gives a feeble smile and doesn't answer. Kader sits down. "That's the boat I'll take when I leave."

Boualem looks mockingly at his younger brother. "Oh yeah? And who'll look after the house?"

Kader launches into his plan, though he knows Hanifa and Boualem always manage to hamper his projects, so he doesn't kid himself too much.

"You can be the one who looks after the house! I'll be the one who goes off to earn foreign currency and you'll be the one in charge here, and when I return in five years' time we'll go into the taxi business. You know, one of those Toyotas, the twelve-seater jobs, fifteen if you squash up. A return journey to Ouida once a week . . ."

Boualem interrupts, "Yes! I know. But, Kader, don't forget, I'll be leaving before you. You're still young. You'll need to eat lots and lots of potatoes to get big and strong."

Kader is aghast by what his brother has just said. "What? You want to leave? You?"

Boualem is embarrassed. "Why not? I'm thinking about it."

Kader gets up to take out one of the hooks. "Just to mess up my plans."

Boualem bursts out laughing. A forced laugh. "Mess up your plans! You must be joking, Kader. At thirteen, you think you can go off, just like that, to work and live elsewhere, all alone. You'll continue at school and then we'll see. You know that's what we decided with Hanifa. You're the one who's got to get to be an engineer at least. I'll be the one sending home the money from abroad."

Kader angrily throws his line into the water.

"I've landed in a family that does nothing but wreck my plans."

Boualem shifts his attention to the ship heading for the open sea. Since yesterday's tryst the loudspeaker problem has moved down the list of his concerns into second place. He has understood finally that the possibility of his marrying Yamina is remote because of his job. The wage he brings home from work is just barely enough to feed the family. And then where would they live? They are in the same dilemma as thousands of young people. Yet most of them, despite living on top of one another, don't hesitate to get married and have children. Boualem thinks that the best and most realistic solution for him is to leave the country. As soon as possible. Dozens of young men from the neighborhood have already left. Of course, some returned rather quickly but others were able to slot into the right channels. They went up north. As far away as possible. And they are still there. They work as best they can and solve their problems as they go along. Boualem knows they will help him once he takes his decision.

But will he be able to live far from Yamina? Will he be able to stand being alone, without her? And will she be able to understand his decision? Here, at least, he feels her closeness, even if he sees her only rarely. If he were bolder he would go up to the terrace more often at night. Before, when they were younger, it was the place where they could make contact, she behind her window and he on the terrace. They had invented a language of gestures, which they alone understood: the terrace telephone. But those were only adolescents' games that ended up becoming dangerous. Boualem smiles vaguely. He has never touched Yamina's skin. It's unbelievable. At his age. He is almost ashamed.

He closes his eyes and tries to imagine the film of his wedding. The *chaabi* orchestra. Mandolins. Banjos. Derboukas. The ululations. The henna. The *burnous*. The friends having a good laugh around the mound of couscous and him in his corner dying of fright. Afraid of being impotent. Who knows? With all the spells and different hatreds. Yamina would be in her room. Somewhat tearful. Wonderfully beautiful in her white dress. Wearing light makeup. Sitting on the edge of the matrimonial bed. Waiting to be taken in his arms. Admiring the beautiful wedding ring on her trembling finger.

And naturally enough, at about midnight, led by a few of his close friends, he would come to cross the threshold and go down the corridor leading toward her, he would begin by gazing at her and then gradually allow his hand to stray on her hair, without being afraid. Perfectly natural. She would smile at him and her lips would part slightly. Her hair would be undone and he would draw near to her face. And Ouardya, leaning against the wall, crying, in the darkness. But what is Ouardya doing here? Is she going to spoil everything? Why is she here in this room? Looking so strange? And this sad smile . . . And why is Imam Rabah suddenly starting to bawl out his sermon? Boualem opens his eyes. Kader observes him, amused.

"When you're asleep you laugh, you make faces. A real Mickey Mouse!"

Boualem shrugs off these confused thoughts by rapidly reciting a verse of the Holy Koran, then lights a cigarette and continues watching the ship, tiny now in the middle of the sea. His lower lip trembles slightly.

24

AN ACRID SMELL OF SWEAT FILLS THE ROOM. THE WALLS COATED WITH shiny white paint reflect the shadows of thirty or so fitness enthusiasts. Here people are working out seriously and in silence. Each one is busy developing his muscles, keeping his body in shape. A few crumpled photographs are pinned to the walls. Taken from magazines, they depict well-known sports figures and advocate the benefits of keeping fit. The coach, a giant with a long beard, his forehead marked by signs of extremely regular prayers, is offering his advice, helped by two assistants sporting impressive muscles. The large mirror entirely covering one of the walls is the focal point for nearly everyone. Eyes fixed on their own reflection, they admire themselves and carefully watch for signs of muscular development.

Saïd, wearing a T-shirt and sweatpants, is rhythmically lifting two large weights. He is panting and sweating profusely. Since becoming a fundamentalist believer, he has become a fervent partisan of the body beautiful. He assiduously attends this gymnasium, which only accepts militants and sympathizers. When he can, he also participates in the summer camps in the quiet coves where the young men are indoctrinated with the joy and love of nature. Saïd loves these moments where he can assess his capacities, observe the development of his muscles, admire the suffering that lines his face when the going gets hard. "Religion recommends sport! You develop your body and strengthen your spirit! Then when you've got to lay into someone, it's being strong that will save you . . ." These sessions also enable him to release his excess violence, help reassure him, and make him feel he can face up to any kind of problem.

Rashid bursts into the room looking completely distraught. He frantically looks around him. When he finally sees Saïd, he rushes towards him, greets him, and whispers, "*Salaam a'leikoum,* Saïd! I've got to talk to you . . ."

Seeing Rashid's agitated state, Saïd is rather frightened. He puts down his weights and leaps to his feet.

"Nothing serious?"

Rashid looks at the ceiling, and stammers, embarrassed, "It's about your sister Yamina and Boualem . . ."

Saïd turns pale. "Yamina!"

A swift glance around tells Rashid that no one is interested in their conversation.

"They were in the church of Notre Dame d'Afrique!"

Saïd is shattered. What Rashid has just told him has hit him harder than a hail of punches. He suddenly feels faint. Groggy. Able only to grab hold of his friend by his shirt collar and shake him. "What were they doing?"

Seeing the devastating effect of his words, Rashid hesitates. He now regrets having got involved in this miserable affair where he has ended up with the tale-teller's role. But it is too late now to draw back. He has to see it through, to remind himself how much he hates Boualem and desires Yamina.

He stammers, "They . . . they were talking. I . . . I got as near as I could . . . I wouldn't swear to it, but I thought they were talking about the loudspeaker. And then some people, some *gouars* arrived. I wouldn't swear to it, but it was sort of arranged. And there was an old woman there who looked like the devil himself . . . Things are bad!"

Saïd takes him to the locker room. An uneasy silence falls between the two men. Rashid suddenly feels weighed down by his act. He can't, daren't look up. He looks unseeingly at the damp tiles in the locker room. Saïd quickly removes his clothes and slips into the shower. Rashid wavers. He wishes he were anywhere but there. He will never forgive himself for the base act he has just committed. How can he, the fighter pure as driven snow, a noble spirit, how can he have fallen so dreadfully low, have been blinded by his troubled feelings, and have played the filthy informer? Saïd calms himself down, blows and splutters, relaxes under the stream of water. He has registered the information and is gradually returning to his senses. He turns off the tap.

"And what exactly were you doing in the church?"

Rashid answers hastily, taken aback by the question. "I wasn't in the church. You know that once a week I meet with the children from the school in front of Notre Dame d'Afrique. It was just chance. I happened to see Boualem go into the church and I followed him in. Yamina was there."

"Yamina was not there!"

Saïd screams it out. Rashid looks at him, terrified. Saïd hurls his towel down on the bench. Making a superhuman effort, Rashid looks up at him. "What d'you mean, she wasn't there?"

Saïd yells even louder, "I'm telling you she wasn't there! Got that? This goes no further. What really matters is that you heard the bastard talking about the loudspeaker. So he's the guilty one! This problem will be solved. By God, it'll be solved."

Rashid gets up, almost pleased with the solution suggested by Saïd. "As for Yamina, the bitch, forget her, she can get stuffed, along with all women put on this earth by the devil himself to cause turmoil in the hearts of men. I'm not going to trouble my brain with trivialities anymore."

Rashid vows to mind his own business from now on. He makes toward the door, muttering to himself, "You're right! What really matters is the loudspeaker!"

25

MESS HESITATED FOR A LONG TIME BEFORE FINALLY DECIDING TO COME to Mabrouk's assigned meeting-place. He has decided to use his meager savings to buy some clothes for the day of his long-awaited return to France, as it is always preferable to look presentable in such circumstances to get past the frontier police and customs.

Mess and Mabrouk meet on a terrace high up in the old neighborhood of the Casbah. The old city built by the Turks, with its houses and their terraces leaning against one other, tumbles untidily down to the port. This sunny afternoon blankets, sheets, and carpets are spread out on all the terraces like a kind of enormous multicolored patchwork contrasting strongly with the dirty white color of the houses. Right at the back, behind the oily waters of the port, the bay of Algiers stretches as far as the eye can see right across to the cape of Tamentefoust.

Moussa, a young teenager with a cigarette hanging from his mouth, sets out a row of brightly colored shirts on the parapet of the terrace. He works with Mabrouk selling off small smuggled articles. Mess has removed his parka and is trying on a red-checked shirt over his white *qamis*. Mabrouk is drinking a can of Tuborg beer. It is his third, so he is perspiring freely. He burps and pats his stomach, hoping this will activate his digestion.

"Pretty good, eh, emigrant! Touch of class."

"Yeah! I like this brand. The others are for girls."

"Well, you're looking somewhat girlish yourself with your *qamis.*"

Half in jest, Mess jumps on his friend, grabs him by the shoulders, and in so doing spills his beer. The two young men romp like children. Mabrouk quickly felt attracted to Mess when he landed in Bab el-Oued but only has a vague idea of his immigration problems.

"Shit! Leave off your crap! Making fun of my *qamis!* I'll bash your head in for you!"

Mabrouk pulls Mess off him.

"You crazy? These houses in the Casbah are pretty shaky! You want us to fall over the edge?"

He wipes off the beer, which has stained his trousers. Young Moussa, unmoved by all this, continues folding shirts. Mess wags his finger at Mabrouk.

"You're overdoing the religion, man!"

Mabrouk stops jesting.

"Well, you're only in it because it suits you."

"That's my business!"

Mess looks longingly at the large ship steaming out to sea. There's a catch in the little emigrant's voice.

"I'll be off soon and won't have to see your effing faces anymore."

Mabrouk uses the opportunity to say something important. "While we're at it, why're you always hanging around Saïd?"

Mess gets annoyed. He yells, "Hanging around! You must be joking! When I was up shit creek in Algiers, no papers, no nothing . . . expelled from France like a fool . . . Three months sleeping in cardboard boxes behind the Post Office, and those bastards trying to screw my arse every night . . . Well, you weren't there to help me. The Imam was. I shan't forget that as long as I live."

Mabrouk doesn't give up. He wants to have everything out with Mess.

"OK, OK. The Imam helped you, put you up in the mosque. That's only natural, Muslim charity. But Saïd didn't. He didn't lift a finger when you were in the shit, and now he's dragging you into all kinds of crap. It can only end in trouble."

Mess frowns.

"Look! Don't get me all steamed up about Saïd! I'm French anyway. My life is over there!" He points to the sea. "The other side of the deep blue sea. My name is carved on all the trees of Bobigny. They know me in the bars there. In the Courtilières, in the

Quatre Mille. That's where my real mates are. This here is just a little time out. Got it? Time out."

Mabrouk slaps his shoulder affectionately.

"Here, you're not going to cry, are you Mess? Come on, give us the horse racing commentary!"

Mess bursts out laughing. Mabrouk knows just how to handle him. Mess adores mimicking a famous TV commentator. He uses his hand as the microphone and starts commentating a horse race at Auteuil. Moussa doesn't understand what is going on but appreciates the mimicry. Mabrouk pats him on the shoulder.

"Sure you don't want a Tuborg?"

"When I get my passport, I'll go on a blinder. For now I'll just take this shirt."

26

SAÏD, DECKED OUT IN HIS FAVORITE GEAR—LEATHER JACKET WORN over his *qamis* and Adidas on his feet—is looking stern as he strides down the main street of Bab el-Oued, accompanied by Rashid and his usual faithful five militants.

Today they are doing the rounds of the market specializing in the sale of mainly contraband goods. Jammed in between a dark street and a dead end in the lower Casbah, it looks like a hastily erected supermarket. Like an open-air Ali Baba's cave. You can find anything you want there from a large fridge to a throwaway cigarette lighter. Saïd has decided to have a look around just for the sake of it. With the information he has received from Rashid, he now knows the facts. "The dirty bastard! What a cunt! It was bound to be him! Why didn't I think of it before? Who else in the neighborhood is more of a troublemaker than Boualem?"

The previous day Saïd had begun by getting into a towering rage, bashing his head against the wall. It was a double insult. Both the loudspeaker and his own sister. He rushed home immediately after leaving the sports center. Fortunately Yamina was not there. She had gone with her mother to visit an aunt. Saïd grabbed the *boussaadi,* the mountain knife which was used, in his father's lifetime, to cut the throats of chickens and, less frequently, those of the sheep slaughtered for the feast of Aïd. The knife was always kept in the same place in the kitchen, sharpened ready for use. Saïd slipped it into his jacket and went out, ready to punish Boualem once and for all. As for Yamina, her turn would come later. He would be back later to deal with that slut dishonoring the family.

Luckily he was diverted by the call to prayer on the way to the bakery where he was certain to find Boualem. "A sign from heaven. The hour was not yet come for blood to flow." Saïd turned back and went to the mosque. He stayed there for several hours, kneeling in silence, expressionless and tense. In the soothing atmosphere of the deserted mosque his fury evaporated and gave way to reflection. "Why give in to anger? Why kill him? We need to use the loudspeaker affair to set an example. That encounter with Yamina though was something else again. That was more complicated. I must know why. And that French woman, blind and sort of satanic . . . satanical. What a mess." The questions were raining thick and fast in Saïd's poor brain. He was not at all used to this kind of situation. If it had just been a matter of trying to recover the loudspeaker stolen by a petty thief in the neighborhood, the whole problem would have been much simpler. Just a beating up in public and that would be the end of it. That was how they had been punishing pickpockets for some time now. But in this case, because his sister was involved, he couldn't foresee where it might lead.

Could he afford to get into trouble while so many great things were in the offing in Bab el-Oued and even throughout the whole country? The political unrest was growing constantly. The Islamic groups had been proliferating over the last few months and there was talk of creating a new political party. Saïd forced himself to think coolly, to curb his emotions which inevitably led him back to Yamina. "In the name of Allah! What a terrible disgrace! Yamina meeting a young man and foreigners in a church!"

Knowing Rashid would keep his mouth shut, Saïd finally decided he needed a plan. He put the knife back in its place, almost relieved not to have given way to his murderous instincts. In due course, Boualem's turn would come!

AFTER QUESTIONING the young street sellers to no avail, the group of beards climbs back up the dark alleys of the Casbah. They suddenly come face-to-face with Mess who is quite taken aback by this accidental encounter. He tries to conceal the little bag containing the shirt he has just bought. Saïd eyes him suspiciously. "Where've you been?"

Mess stammers, "Just . . . just b . . . been to visit a cousin . . ."

"I didn't know you had a cousin living here . . ."

"Well . . . he's paralyzed . . . never goes out . . ."

Saïd doesn't believe a word. He has caught sight of the bag Mess is hiding behind his back.

"Paralyzed, eh? Well come along with us. We're on our way up to Bab j'did."

Saïd scratches his beard. He secretly thinks, "This crappy little emigrant, looks like butter wouldn't melt in his mouth, got to keep an eye on him . . . You never know what he's thinking, and he still hasn't learnt to speak Arabic though he's been hanging about Algiers long enough. You'd think it was deliberate!" Now things are moving, Saïd is beginning to realize that taking Bab el-Oued in hand with all these unpredictable young men is not that simple. Information from the other neighborhoods, such as Kouba, Belcourt, Bachdjarah, indicates that there is large-scale mobilization under way. "There's a major demonstration being prepared in a stadium at the end of the month; we shall see if there are a lot of young people from Bab el-Oued . . ."

After returning from their unsuccessful visit to the upper Casbah, Saïd and his group cross into the pedestrian city center. From time to time they greet the other beards they meet on their way with a knowing collective salute. By the statue of the Emir Abdelkader, which Saïd detests—*Haram!* That's not the way to honor heroes! Waste of money to pay the Italians to produce that load of crap"—the group catches sight of a pretty young girl wearing makeup and a short skirt, which reveals her charms. Mess cannot help turning round to have a good look. Saïd pounces on his lubricious glance. "Shame on you! You'll burn in hell!"

"Sorry, Saïd! I didn't mean it!"

"Say sorry to the Almighty. Who knows if He'll forgive you?"

Mess, embarrassed, bows his head. Saïd mutters to himself, "It'll take time but I know we'll find the loudspeaker! Don't you worry! We'll find it even if we have to turn the whole city upside down!"

27

HASSAN-THE-BAKER, SITTING BEHIND HIS COUNTER, IS TELLING HIS old friend Aami Mourad for the nth time about his evenings at Padovani's in the old French days, when there was that fantastic atmosphere. The elderly customer greedily devours a third slice of pizza.

Aami Mourad belongs to the generation before Hassan's. He was in the Second World War, has seen the black market and the American landings, has been a militant in the Algerian Communist Party, enjoyed the magnificent celebrations of the Stalin "Father of the masses" cult, the dockers' strikes during the Indochina war, the mass meetings of the nationalist movement, and the excursions to the Sidi Ferruch forest. Vague memories destroyed by deep-seated resentment, unwelcome old age, and a fatal lack of understanding of the present. Aami Mourad thinks that the main responsibility for the crisis affecting the country is "something indefinable, something monstrous we have ourselves created. And this monster will devour us in the end." He is convinced that "Algeria is on the verge of immense upheavals. Tragic events, far worse than what has just been going on in Lebanon. A huge earthquake that will swallow us up." Aami Mourad, who is contradiction personified, after voicing his fears proceeds to proclaim loudly to anyone who wishes to hear that he couldn't care less anyway. As a miserable old pensioner, cast off by his family years before, he has nothing left to hope for. All that remains for him is to watch with a certain morbid pleasure what he calls "the onset of approaching disaster."

Aami Mourad has organized various "observation posts" where he spends time each day pulling to pieces and commenting on his fellow human beings in his nasty way. There is the window of the small cupboard that serves as his home, which is where he looks out from at the end of the day and late into the night. He turns out the light and watches. From there he savors the sight of the concealed breakdown of families, watches his neighbors, spies on their privacy. "Families who don't speak to one another. Who come and go, glide through the rooms like ghosts. And you'd never see any one of them opening a book! Look at them! The women always in their kitchens, bending over taps without water. The men torn between the TV set and their prayers or slumped in their chairs, oblivious to the dreadful racket of the kids who don't know the difference between a football stadium and an apartment."

His second favorite place for spying on people is Hassan's bakery where he spends his mornings gobbling pizzas and resentfully observing "these beggars' huge love of their stomachs"! He counts over and over again the number of loaves each family buys. His morbid accounting bears out his innermost conviction that the population has been transformed into a horde of "guts on legs, manipulated and dominated by the food shortages." In the afternoons he can be found on the benches of Port-Saïd Square, a strategic position near the central bus and taxi station connecting the capital to the rest of the country. A meeting point. "Here I can admire people dragging along their bodies; it's like being in the courtyard of a hospital! We are all sick! That's what we are. Sick! Our energy has evaporated. We're becoming degenerate and don't know it."

Aami Mourad, knowing he is part and parcel of this population, that he belongs to these people who surround him, who are like him, concludes bitterly that he should logically loathe and despise himself as much as he does the others. Day after day, wandering around in this unhealthy atmosphere, symbol of the curse upon the country, Aami Mourad is deliberately killing himself by devouring pizzas—his only food—in order to avoid having to be around for the promised catastrophe. The cancer gnawing inexorably at his stomach, making him scream with pain each night once the windows are closed and the lights turned off, this inescapable disease no longer even troubles him. Aami Mourad had withdrawn into himself well before Independence, during the 1950s, when the FLN unleashed the war of liberation. He felt prematurely old and decided not to participate in the forthcoming struggle. In fact, in some confused way, he had the feeling that an upheaval was brewing that he was not ready to accept. That was the way it was. Yet he had been passionately interested in the war in Indochina. Obviously he supported the Vietminh, but when the storm of decolonization approached the shores of Algeria, he ceased communicating altogether. He turned into a shadow gently wafting through the seven years of war. He was nonetheless arrested because of his Marxist past and spent a few years in a camp during the war. He refused to join the FLN since he was a communist and when Independence arrived it was not a joyful occurrence. Then he moved on to his period of "passive resistance" and of "all-out criticism of the peasants who had taken power and were driving the country to rack and ruin."

He did, however, have one happy interlude. After the riots of October 1988 the Marxist party, which had taken over from the communist party, was legalized. The militants who had come out of hiding had celebrated this in a hall in Algiers. Aami Mourad had put on his blue suit, brushed his hair, and gone along, though he had not been invited. His first political act for more than forty years. He amazed himself. After a few difficulties, since no one knew him, he was allowed in to Ibn Khaldoun hall. A young girl gave him a red rose and he settled down in a seat, tearful, like a child. He recognized a few old militants and was surprised they were still alive. He fell asleep during the secretary general's speech and was woken up by the applause and ululations. A great celebration, the last one, which lightened up his gloomy day-to-day existence. He continued to buy *Alger Républicain,* the newspaper published by the communists, mainly so as to read the page about the problems of the elderly. As for the rest . . .

A child sets off a firecracker near the bakery, which intensely annoys both men. "You maniacs!" yells Aami Mourad. Just then Saïd bursts into the shop, his faithful followers at his side. He immediately adopts an aggressive tone to address Hassan. "Salaam! I'm looking for Mabrouk . . ."

The baker sniffs the musk wafting through the shop. He finds it disgusting when it is so powerful.

"Well, as it happens, when Mabrouk isn't at work, he doesn't actually tell me what he does."

Saïd looks at him disdainfully. He doesn't like Hassan's tone. "You always sound just like the television. Smart aleck, just you wait and see . . ."

He turns around and hurries out of the shop, deliberately leaving his sentence unfinished. He knows that Hassan understands perfectly the threat underlying his words. Hassan shrugs his shoulders.

"My God! How I dislike that guy! He seems to think he's the local policeman!"

Aami also loathes Saïd. He has a laugh and stuffs in another slice of pizza.

"He's just a failure like the others! That's all."

"Yes, but I don't like him. I don't like the way he looks. I don't like the way he speaks. I don't like his beard. I don't like anything about him . . ."

"Well, at any rate, I like your pizzas."

"Yeah!"

Ten minutes later, Boualem comes into the bakery. Nearly every day he passes by in the late afternoon to collect some fresh bread for the evening meal. He finds Hassan and Aami Mourad sprawling on their seats. They look full up and rather queasy. On the counter the empty pizza tray bears witness to the feast that has just taken place. Boualem picks up and eats a forgotten olive. He pretends not to understand. "What's going on?"

Hassan answers groggily, "We bet each other we could stuff down half a slab of pizza in ten minutes. I won! Aami Mourad dropped out after the fifteenth slice . . ." Aami Mourad can barely speak. "Yeah! This evening when I throw up there won't be anyone to look after me . . . Not the first time I've made a stupid bet."

Boualem smiles and goes to the back of the shop.

"OK, I'll take my bread!"

Hassan gets up, does up his trousers, and follows.

"Hey Boualem! Saïd was here just a minute ago looking for Mabrouk. I didn't know they were buddies."

Boualem chooses his loaves from a straw basket. He takes four that look well cooked. "Saïd looking for Mabrouk?" asks Boualem thoughtfully.

"Yes, he came along just now with his gang. Swaggering and rude as ever."

"Well, he's hardly likely to change . . . OK, I'm off. See you later!"

Boualem leaves the shop, somewhat puzzled, wondering why on earth Saïd was looking for Mabrouk.

28

THE DISUSED WAREHOUSE IN THE INDUSTRIAL AREA BY THE SEA, ALONG the road to the airport east of Algiers, is unusually busy today. Fifteen or so young men are swarming around a tarpaulin-covered truck parked in a corner, far from any curious onlookers. Mabrouk is part of the group. A man of about fifty is firmly taking charge of the distribution of a batch of goods which has just arrived from Marseilles (clothes, soaps, crockery, household electrical goods, cigarettes, cheeses). He is in a hurry and gets them to speed things up. Mabrouk fills up his bag. He says good-bye to the man and leaves by way of a long corridor leading to an even bigger hall. Suddenly he finds himself face-to-face with Saïd and his buddies who seem to have emerged from nowhere and are blocking his path. They grab hold of him and hurl him violently against the wall. While two of them hold him fast, Rashid empties the contents of his bag. Jeans, shirts, soaps, boxes of cheese, panties, and bras spill out on the ground.

Mabrouk, stunned by this attack, is paralyzed by fear. He puts up no resistance. Saïd snatches the Walkman attached to his belt and smashes it against the wall.

"Well, then, baker's-boy? Making a bit on the side, are we? As you see, we know everything about you."

Mabrouk stammers, "What . . . what do you want?"

Saïd, in a low, threatening voice, says, "From you? Nothing. It's your pal Boualem we're interested in. The one who goes into churches."

"I . . . I don't understand."

Rashid starts laughing. Mess and the others follow suit. Saïd pulls back Mabrouk's head and adds tauntingly, "We'll make you understand. You will tell us everything you know about the stolen loudspeaker. And we know you know."

Mabrouk rallies all his strength and yells so loudly he startles his aggressors. Seizing his opportunity, he wrests himself free and starts running down the corridor. Saïd and his companions, once they have recovered from their surprise, are hard on his heels. After a mad dash, Mabrouk finds himself in the main hall of the warehouse where the covered lorry had been parked. The hall is now totally empty. Mabrouk is terrified. He is fat and cannot run very fast, and the others soon catch up with him. A few kicks and punches and he caves in.

"Now you're going to spit it all out. You can go on with your *trabendo* afterward. We're not against trade. What we are against is the bastards who get in our way."

Mabrouk tries to protect his face against this latest onslaught. Mess stands aside. He is pale and cannot bear to watch.

"Feeling faint, are we, Mess? Afraid of getting our hands dirty?"

Saïd watches Mabrouk being beaten up, satisfied with his little trick. The militants now know who the culprit is and Mabrouk has become the informer. The first part of Saïd's plan has worked. Rashid looks at him with satisfaction, nodding as if he were reading his friend's thoughts. "Our next victim will be Boualem!"

29

LALLA JAMILA IS BUSY AT HER SEWING MACHINE MAKING LITTLE DRESSES. Someone knocks at the door. She gets up and goes to open it. She is surprised to see Paulo and his blind aunt, standing smiling in the corridor. Paulo is clutching a bouquet of flowers, which he gives to Yamina's mother.

"Good morning, Madame! My name is Paulo Gasen and this is my aunt, Arlette Victoire Gasen."

Yamina's mother hesitates.

"Good morning to you both!"

The aunt takes a step forward, eager to enter the apartment. "Good morning, Madame. We don't want to disturb you."

"Come in! You're not disturbing me."

Lalla Jamila steps aside and lets them in. Inside the apartment Paulo takes a good look around.

"Oh, Auntie! If only you could see! Nothing has changed!"

Noticing the surprise of Lalla Jamila, Paulo attempts to explain.

"I must tell you. We used to live here before. Well, that is to say, my aunt did. I lived on the other side of the road."

Lalla Jamila, who has finally understood what they are talking about, smiles.

"Oh, I see, you were the people living here before . . . Delighted to meet you . . ."

She calls out, "Yamina! Yamina!"

"We're on a kind of pilgrimage," adds Paulo.

Yamina appears, a saucepan in her hand.

"What is it?"

"Say hello to our guests and prepare us some coffee."

Recognizing the people she saw in the church, Yamina blushes, but she recovers quickly. She smiles at Paulo.

"Hello!"

Her mother hands over the flowers to Yamina as she leaves the room. Lalla Jamila clears away the little dresses piled up on the sofa.

"Please sit down!"

Paulo and his aunt sit down.

"I didn't know your family because we lived at Madame d'Afrique. We came to live here in 1963."

"Well, for most of my life I lived in this house with poor old Christopher."

Tears roll down her cheeks.

"Oh, Auntie! You're not going to cry, are you?"

"Let her have a little cry if she wants to! It does you good now and again; I can understand that. Please make yourselves at home. If you would like to show her around . . ."

Paulo gives his aunt a little handkerchief. She wipes her eyes. "We're spending three or four days in Algiers. We're staying at the Aletti hotel. My aunt so wanted to make this trip here and so did I, though I'm so busy at work . . ."

He takes a small white card out of his pocket and gives it to Lalla Jamila with a theatrical gesture. The grating sound of a key turning in the lock interrupts what Paulo was about to say. The front door slams and a few seconds later Saïd bursts into the room. When he sees Paulo and his aunt he hesitates, then, with a frown, asks his mother, "Who are this lot here?"

Lalla Jamila, noticing Saïd's belligerent tone, attempts an embarrassed smile before answering, "They're the people who lived here before. Say good morning."

Saïd speaks loud and fast.

"Why have they come back? Have they forgotten something?"

Paulo hasn't understood Saïd's words. He holds out his hand. Saïd pretends not to see it. He turns away, then leaves the room angrily. The front door slams violently. Paulo smiles, embarrassed.

"Bit touchy, the young man."

"Don't bother about him. That's my son, he's a real rough one."

Yamina comes back into the room carrying a large tray with coffee and cakes. She puts it down on the low table. Mme Gasen is fidgety. She taps her cane on the ground.

"Can I see the terrace?"

Lalla Jamila begins serving the coffee. "But of course. After you've had your coffee."

Behind her dark glasses the old lady's emotion is obvious as she nods sadly.

"The number of sweaters I knitted, up there . . ."

Paulo eyes the cakes.

"They look good! *Mantekaos* cakes! I love them!"

Yamina smiles at him. "My mother's specialty."

LALLA JAMILA, the blind aunt, and Paulo are on the terrace, already colonized by Hanifa and her friends, busy doing their washing.

"Good morning ladies! It's a beautiful day . . ."

The women are intimidated by Paulo's intrusion into their private territory.

"Good morning!"

"We don't want to disturb you. We just wanted to admire the view."

"These people used to be our neighbors. They lived here before. In the French era."

Paulo guides his aunt toward the edge of the terrace. Hanifa lashes out with her sharp tongue, "Poor things! They've come back to see this Mickey Mouse city!"

Lynda swiftly conceals the books she was about to exchange.

"How dreadful!" continues one of the girls, in the same vein.

Lalla Jamila, irritated, shrugs her shoulders.

"You lot of backbiters! Always criticizing, never doing anything constructive."

"I don't see what we could do. We're never allowed to say anything . . ."

"For a start, you could do your washing more carefully without letting the dirty water flood the terrace as you usually do . . . Well! I'm off. Back to my sewing. I'm not going to let you all get on my nerves."

She goes up to Paulo.

"Mr. Paulo, before leaving do call in again and I'll prepare some *mantekaos* cakes for you."

"Thank you ! We won't be staying long."

When Lalla Jamila leaves, the women burst out laughing all together. Hanifa mimics her.

"Just let me just prepare a few *mantekaos* cakes for you . . . I bet she'll sell them for some hard currency!"

"You've got a really nasty mind!"

Paulo, indifferent to the agitation on the terrace, begins to describe the view.

"If you could only see the view, Auntie! All the blocks of flats are dazzlingly white. They look wonderful against the blue sky. Fantastic! If I were a painter, I'd come here for inspiration . . ."

Hanifa and the women have suddenly ceased their bantering. They observe Paulo and his aunt in silence. Hanifa is amazed at what the man is saying.

"He must be cracked! He's telling her the buildings are all white. That it's all beautiful. I don't believe it . . ."

"Can't he see how dirty and decrepit everything is?" wonders Lynda.

"Not that surprising! The woman can't see. She's blind. He doesn't want to upset her," adds Hannane.

Zobra, the fourth-floor neighbor, approves of Paulo's approach.

"I think he's right!"

That triggers off another round of discussion among the women.

"He sees what he wants to see . . ."

"In any case, one thing is true in what he's been saying. The sky really is blue . . ."

They burst out laughing. Hanifa looks at Paulo with a hint of lust in her eyes.

"He's a good-looking man. Just the kind I need. He'd get me across the sea and I wouldn't have to see this wretched country and your dismal faces anymore. I'd become queen of Paris."

Lynda gives her a book.

"Huh! You feeling OK? Tell Kader to read you this book tonight. That'll give you something to think about."

"Nah, I don't read that rubbish."

The muezzin's call to prayer puts an end to the discussion. The women disperse immediately. They go straight to their apartments for the prayer.

30

THE MOSQUE IS OVERFLOWING WITH PEOPLE. THE FAITHFUL, AS EVERY Friday, are both inside and outside the building. Saïd and his little group are slightly apart. On the other side of the great hall Boualem is sitting beside Hassan-the-baker. At the back, hidden behind a column, the mysterious fair-haired man with the signet ring and the BMW is gazing into space. The congregation is listening carefully to the sermon of Imam Rabah.

"Our city needs peace and calm. What we saw in October, all the dead and wounded, all those children cut down in their prime, should make us think about the way we live. Islam is a religion of tolerance. We should banish violence. We must convince the others . . ."

Saïd turns round slowly. He stares discreetly at Boualem, who, sensing his gaze, raises his head. Saïd is surprised. He is forced to meet Boualem's eyes. For a few seconds the two young men weigh each other up and wage a silent but merciless battle. Saïd gives way first. He turns away and concentrates on the Imam's words.

"The Islamic solution for our country will take place through the will of the majority. We must convince them. Keep on and on. Never give up. This is the only way we can carry our ideas forward . . ."

Imam Rabah is starting to become troubled. Yet he had felt so at home in this neighborhood. "Thanks be to God!" as he was wont to murmur.

He had settled here two years before, at the age of forty-five, and for him this new city-dweller's life was a revelation. "All positive, thanks to Allah!" Ten years earlier he was leading the prayers in a small village mosque somewhere in the Aurès mountains. Once a month he went to the big city. There he met an old blind sheikh, a disciple of some Egyptian Islamists. The sheikh took him under his wing and made him his pupil. He taught him the complexity of life, of religion, without forgetting the "political dialectic which is absolutely necessary in a crisis-ridden Algeria, bubbling with ideas, a spawning ground for all sorts of different experiments and in search of its identity."

Through the network of militants patiently set up by the "brothers," Imam Rabah was noticed for his magnanimity, his commitment, his honesty, and his knowledge of religion. They contacted him and he was offered the chance to be in charge in the new mosque of Bab el-Oued. For him Bab el-Oued was a bit like China, a far-off country full of mysteries and dangers. Imam Rabah was abnormally suspicious of the unknown. And everything he was told about the depraved capital, where there was alcoholism, prostitution, Marxism, and fraud, was enough to make him hesitate.

The messenger, an old inhabitant of Algiers, took several days to convince him, boasting to him of the past, present, and future importance of this particular neighborhood of Algiers. The Imam, pretending to be curious, asked him countless questions, intending to catch out his envoy so he could be left in peace in his village. But this was wasted effort, since the envoy had an answer to everything. He was a cunning old fellow who claimed to "know the city like the back of his hand and love it so much that he could if he wanted write a book on each neighborhood, from the Casbah to Belcourt, from Bologhine to El Harrach, taking in El Biar and Bouzaréah on the way. A book which would be three times as thick as the telephone book."

"You'll see!" he kept on repeating, "it's an engaging working-class neighborhood where you will feel at home. Bab el-Oued, you know, has had an especially rich and stormy past. It was an old bastion of Spanish, Maltese, and Italian workers, a haven for exiled members of the Commune, a watering hole for the ritual alcoholic drink of anisette—may Allah protect us—and for the waves of laughter on a Sunday morning . . ."

Imam Rabah never understood why the emissary from Algiers, carried away by his theme, bothered to mention the drinking of anisette and the waves of laughter on a Sunday morning. Sometimes the ins and outs of human logic are so tortuous . . .

"Bab el-Oued ends at the old naval district with its famous El Anka Café, a great name in the popular music of Algiers, and the hill of Basséta, next to the Climat de France, sarcastically called 'Climat de Souffrance,' or the climate of suffering. That is because of its sordid housing estates dominated by the different neighborhoods: Beau Fraisier, Carrière Jaubert, and Notre Dame d'Afrique. Bab el-Oued has seen many upheavals always surprisingly connected to the political situation of the country. It was a communist—may God protect us and keep us from evil—haven at the beginning of the century, and later on became almost naturally the stamping ground for the terrorist activities of the OAS ultras and commandos at the end of the war of Independence. After the *pieds-noirs* left en masse—and may Allah not bring them back—it was just as naturally taken over by the inhabitants of the shanty towns thronging the hills nearby and also by the people swarming in from the countryside. You'll like it, you'll see . . .

"Later on, Bab el-Oued, forgotten by the new masters of the country, just like most other popular districts of Algiers, witnessed in rapid succession our entry into the Third World, the birth of the new bourgeoisie of peasant origin, the flourishing of corruption, government intervention, and widespread mediocrity. All it could then do was to develop its own way of thinking and its own survival mechanisms, while gradually becoming a natural extension of the Casbah, another equally historic neighborhood also on the verge of rapid decline and general disrepair. But you'll like it, you'll see . . ."

What the envoy did not bother to spell out was that Bab el-Oued, as it happened, was one of the first districts of the capital to be taken in hand, patiently and methodically, by the Islamists who emerged in the 1970s, while the famous "specific socialism" of Colonel Boumédienne was evaporating in the cries, tears, and general hysteria of the burial of the nationalistic leader. Following a few discreet battles for the empty seat of power, the Algeria of that time was soon to appear, despite a veneer of stability, in all the horror of its corrupt, unsuccessful reality. Schooling, culture, everyday life, morality, nationalism, like rotten fruit falling off a tree, were all about to burst apart in the fury of the 1980s.

This was how Bab el-Oued, the neighborhood of constant deprivation, of pride despite poverty, of macho honor, of contempt and social exclusion; how Bab el-Oued, the neighborhood of the oil poor as opposed to the oil rich, came, on October 1988—a day ahead of everyone else—to be in the vanguard of the major riots that were suddenly going to turn the towns and countryside of Algeria into a bloodbath and lead to an irreversible split. And, naturally, Bab el-Oued paid the highest toll in terms of the children and young people mown down by bullets or savagely tortured during the ensuing repression.

The Islamists, losing no time coming out of hiding, had naturally understood the political capital to be reaped from the spirit of rebellion and the unrest and aimlessness of the young men sickened and angry at the now disgraced state. This was the state that had sown corruption and caused underdevelopment, which was the mouthpiece of the ubiquitous FLN, now grown into a huge bureaucratic monster.

IMAM RABAH, won over in the end by the envoy, landed in Bab el-Oued one winter's morning. They found him a small garret where he could move in with his few belongings and his books. He took over the Hayat mosque, which, like thousands of other mosques scattered throughout the country, was continually being added to, thanks to gifts and collections. The law in fact allowed mosques to remain free as long as they remained unfinished. Free meant that they were placed under the control of a religious or charitable association and were not subject to the diktat of the Ministry of Religion, which obliged the Imam-in-office to read an official sermon.

Imam Rabah got to know the faithful of his neighborhood and gradually got used to the city. His only cause of bother was the damp sea air, which aggravated his chronic sinusitis.

31

BEFORE THE BEGINNING OF THE PRAYERS IMAM RABAH HAD ASKED Saïd to join him afterwards in the reading room of the mosque. Saïd did not know what the Imam wanted. "That Imam, he's getting a bit above himself and I don't like it! He's not even from Algiers!" Saïd was still a little worried because as a rule the Imam left him alone. He wondered what he could possibly want from him today. Saïd was convinced that the Imam didn't like him, and it was mutual. Their views of Islam were diametrically opposed: Imam Rabah didn't at all like the agitator side to him. The Imam was, of course, a fundamentalist, but he always thought about the situations that arose, analyzing them and weighing them up before taking action, whereas Saïd, in his knee-jerk way, always tended to pitch in without looking about him first.

That was how, during the first march of the Islamists, during the October riots, Imam Rabah was part of the group against that initiative, considering it too dangerous in such a turbulent period. Saïd, though, had not hesitated for a single moment to participate in the march and was even in the front line of the demonstrators. That was the day before he was arrested. When the shooting started, opposite the police headquarters, Imam Rabah flew into a violent rage, shouting that there had been provocation and blaming the irresponsible leaders who would be accountable to the Almighty for the bloodshed. As for Saïd, he threw himself on the ground when he heard the bullets whistling around him, thinking,

"Shit! This is scary!" But he still claimed it had been a good idea to have a march.

The reading room of the mosque is a small, clean, white-washed room just behind the building. Its only ornament is a modest book cabinet filled with large books provided or purchased by Imam Rabah. This was where Mess slept when he was taken in by the Imam. At that time the young emigrant was living on a knife edge, completely paranoid, terrified of the many dangers that the night might conceal. Each time Imam Rabah came to see him after the final prayer and sat down quite naturally on the edge of the mattress, Mess felt his stomach tense up. "OK, OK, so I know he's a man of religion, but he could just as well be one of those night rapists." Imam Rabah understood his fears and patiently gained the young man's confidence through his kindness and advice.

The Imam is sitting on a mat. He adjusts a pair of spectacles on his nose, then reads in a low voice a few suras from the Holy Book open on his knees. Saïd has sat down opposite him. He can't stop fidgeting, stroking his beard, and cracking his fingers. "He's keeping me waiting on purpose! And what's more he has smelly feet!" To overcome his nervousness Saïd is trying to convince himself that the Imam is a pathetic nonentity. He looks at him and secretly sneers at his provincial way of wearing the *keffiyeh,* at his glasses stuck together with sticking plaster, at the traces of small-pox on his face. "He could have stayed in his little *jebels!* As if we didn't have enough suitable people in Algiers to be Imam. They always want to bring in some outsider. He's drawing it out a bit. He's pretending to read but is really thinking about what he's going to say to me. Zerma! He thinks he's in a Hitchcock film." Unable to stand it any longer, he loudly cracks one of his fingers. The Imam raises his eyes and smiles kindly. He closes the Koran and hugs it to his chest. His voice is gentle.

"I don't much like the news I've received!"

Saïd shifts uncomfortably.

"What news?"

The Imam takes off his glasses, folds them up, and carefully wraps them up in a cotton rag.

"Saïd! You know perfectly well what I'm talking about. The loudspeaker. You spend your time attacking people, threatening them, and you've even hit someone."

"But sheikh! We must find the loudspeaker. We only attack those who deserve it. Can't you see what's happening in this neighborhood? The young men are laughing at us."

"I know, I know! But things can be done without violence."

"What matters is results. I've got to find that loudspeaker."

The Imam smiles once again, as if he were addressing someone mentally deficient.

"We have precisely fifteen loudspeakers on the terraces. Do you really think having one less is a problem?"

Saïd, outraged at this, gets up.

"I can't see what you're getting at. And in any case, I now know who's responsible."

He turns away and leaves the room. Imam Rabah watches him leave without restraining him. He takes up the Koran once more and opens it.

"Violence begets violence!"

32

A TAXI IS DRIVING AT TOP SPEED ALONG THE COAST ROAD LEADING TO the beaches west of Algiers. Alilou, the driver, is a young man in the *redjla* style of Bab el-Oued. He enjoys having a laugh, telling stories, all of which he swears are true but can never be verified. Sex is their main subject. Mabrouk, Boualem, and three other friends of his are piled into the vehicle, a masterpiece of kitsch style, covered with stickers, pins, curtains, miniature fans, Spanish dolls, a little cloth embroidered with "Home Sweet Home," an imitation carphone, and an immense loudspeaker connected to the car radio. To liven up their outing to the beach Alilou is telling them of his latest adventure.

"I look in the mirror and see this stunning woman taking off her *hidjab*. She folds and stuffs it in her bag. And what do I see? A real sex-bomb, with eyes like Kim Basinger in *Nine-and-a-Half Weeks*, and boobs! Wow! Heart attack, car crash, you name it, I was in for it! Then she says, 'How about it?' I answered, 'You bet!' She says, 'Are you ready?' I was on fire! I change down, turn around, and head straight for the zoo. Fuck me, but there's not a free spot anywhere for a quick shag! You'd think the whole of Algiers had a date there. No one admiring the animals, but in the woods, not a single tree unoccupied . . . Like an open-air brothel! I'd heard about it but I didn't believe it."

"So what did you do?"

"Nothing, that day! But the rest of the story is longer and more complicated than the *Thousand and One Nights*. I'll tell you the next installment on Friday . . ."

The taxi is almost at Franco beach.

THE GROUP MEETS UP in a bar run by Bob-the-Jap. This amusing character has never set foot in Japan but everyone calls him the Jap in tribute to a hazy karate past. He's a hunk of a man who looks like a child except for a long scar running across his tanned face. His draught beer is a specialty attracting consumers from all parts of Algiers. The absolute height of refinement is that the beer is served here in mugs imported from Alsace.

Behind his bar the skinny, spotty barman, acting blasé, fills the glasses and removes the froth from the beer at top speed to satisfy the clients' unquenchable thirst. Bob-the-Jap serves the beers, moving from one table to another, providing constant patter to keep people happy. Alilou knows him well. From time to time, he deals with him when he is able to winkle out a few bottles of whisky or Ricard.

"Nice and cold, is it, then, Jap?"

"Sure thing!"

"Give us five beers and a mineral water for Boualem. He's not drinking today!"

Alilou bursts out laughing, pleased at his wit. Bob-the-Jap laughs too, then lets rip a karate cry. Enough, with the help of the alcohol, to provoke general hilarity. Alilou takes off his shirt.

"I'm going to down a couple of iced beers to cool off, then I'm going in the water. Hey, Jap boy, not too much froth there!"

In the group only Mabrouk is gloomy. As a result of his encounter with Saïd and his gang he has bruises on his cheeks and behind his ears. He doesn't say much, and when Bob-the-Jap brings the beers he drinks his in one go. Boualem watches him, then slaps him on the shoulder.

"Seems to be going down OK! You drowning your sorrows?"

Mabrouk turns his head away. He signals to the Jap to bring him another beer. Alilou and the others soon empty their mugs, then get up and go out, burping, toward a shed behind the bar. They put on their bathing trunks and go down to the rocks. Alone now with Mabrouk, Boualem persists.

"You've got something to tell me and can't get it out."

Mabrouk sniffs.

"I, well, it's the loudspeaker. They know it's you. Yesterday they got hold of me and made me spit out what they wanted. They're dangerous. They already knew it was you."

Boualem smiles at him.

"Don't worry! They're pathetic. So they beat you up?"

Mabrouk pulls a face.

"Can't you see? I hurt all over."

"The bastards! They're strong when they're in a gang."

"And what's more—it's even worse—they say that now you go to churches and meet up with foreigners. That drives Saïd just crazy. From his eyes I could see he was ready to kill."

Hearing Mabrouk's last words Boualem suddenly feels worried. A shiver runs through his body. Anxiety floods through him . . . Who could have seen him in the church? If they saw him, they must have seen Yamina. His head is pounding. He feels that it is about to begin again. His skull is exploding. Endless complications . . . Mabrouk realizes that Boualem is completely shaken by what he has just heard. He looks at him with some sympathy.

"They've decided to give you a hard time! I told you it was a fucking stupid thing to do!"

Boualem rips off his T-shirt and gets up.

"I'm going for a swim! Have another beer, on me!"

33

FRIDAY EVENINGS, THE LAST DAY OF THE WEEK, ARE ALWAYS GLOOMY and long drawn out in Algiers. People feel uneasy once night has fallen. They halfheartedly get ready for another working week. The city empties even more quickly than it does on other evenings. Bab el-Oued is no exception. The bluish light of television screens flickers through most of the neighborhood, the only permitted escape from a joyless weekend. The block of flats at 13 Ramdane-Kahlouche Street does not have a satellite dish and the tenants who want one have linked up with the block opposite, number 14. They paid three thousand dinars and bingo! one evening they had six TV channels instead of one. Great rejoicing! Initially people were somewhat reluctant, but, being curious, more and more viewers soon wanted the extra channels.

Lalla Jamila, at Yamina's insistence, agreed to a linkup as long as Saïd didn't find out. That was not difficult as he never went near the television now that he had discovered religion. At the beginning he had even tried to sell the television set. But his mother warned him that if he touched it, he'd get the frying pan over his head. Since then the six foreign channels, in French, English, and

German, were available in Lalla Jamila's home, creating, here as elsewhere, new problems because of the many programs and especially the "indecent pictures."

In every family where the men had agreed to have the satellite link, consensus was necessary. Those who could afford it bought a second television set for the men only; the others, which was most families, had to take turns. The adolescents were almost always excluded. They stayed in the streets or under the porch of the blocks of flats until the programs were over.

Lalla Jamila and Yamina loved the games and soaps. This Friday evening they had a quick supper, did the washing up, and settled down in the sitting room. Yamina's mother used the time to tack a few dresses. After listening to the weather forecast and the ads, the fifth part of *The Thorn Birds* was about to begin. Saïd was no doubt hanging around somewhere outside, and the younger brother, as usual, was at the neighbors' who were very keen on watching an American crime series broadcast at the same time on another channel. Lalla Jamila and Yamina couldn't wait because they adored their soap. After a few moments they were carried away, in the thick of the plot, sharing the betrayals, passions, and sufferings and swooning at the appearance of their heartthrob. The spellbinding voice of Richard Chamberlain transported them far from Bab el-Oued, far from Algiers, far from Algeria. For a whole hour, the two women felt they were alive.

They just barely heard the sound of a key turning in the lock. Yamina leaped up and changed the program. Instead of the soap, a round table on politics, broadcast by Algerian television, appeared on the screen, the kind of program that takes up a whole evening and makes you feel deeply depressed. Lalla Jamila pricks her finger and grumbles, "That's him! Trust him to always arrive at the wrong moment!"

Saïd bursts into the sitting room and shifts nervously from one foot to the other, making his flip-flops squeak. He immediately looks at the TV screen, where two politicians, members of the FLN, are flattering one another and proffering banalities. Saïd says sarcastically, "You think I don't know what you were watching, along with all the other idiots in this neighborhood? Just you wait, one day we'll burn down your satellite dish!"

Without waiting for an answer he about-turns, goes, and locks himself into his room. A powerful voice fills the sitting room. Before going to sleep, Saïd listens to a cassette of an inflammatory sermon he has just got from Constantine. Fuming, Lalla Jamila signals to Yamina. "Well, come on! Put the film back on. It'll be hard to follow the story now."

34

THIS SATURDAY MORNING THE WHOLE NEIGHBORHOOD HAS SLOWED down because of the heat wave. People move around avoiding the areas in the sun. Ammar the postman, who, at forty-five, wonders every day why he continues to do this stupid job delivering letters to fools, is finding it hard work climbing up the stairs in the block of flats. He grunts and sweats. The tenants pay him a small sum of money to bring up their mail since their mailboxes downstairs have been useless for a long time. First their post was stolen each day, or if not it was burned by the kids. Then the letterboxes were all methodically vandalized until they were no more than gaping shelves used to dump bits of dried bread since bread—food of the Almighty—must never be left lying on the ground.

ONCE HE HAS REACHED the fifth story Ammar makes straight for the door of one of the apartments. He loves this one. He rejoices and gives thanks to heaven for starting his week with this flat. He takes a letter from his bag, then knocks gently. The door is opened slightly, revealing a tall, slim platinum blonde with large black made-up eyes. The *femme fatale* of Bab el-Oued. A magic moment for Ammar the postman. Intense tantalizing pleasure. Beautiful discreet Lamia. Though, for Ammar, the secrets of the attractive Lamia are far from secret since he discovered by chance that she was . . ."The bitch! I know all about her. She doesn't fool me!"

Officially, Lamia is a nurse at the Maillot hospital. However, to double her wages, she dances three nights a week in a cabaret at Bouzaréah. Ammar went there, taken along by a friend. He saw her and almost swooned with delight at her sensual, provocative belly dancing. Since then, he can't get it out of his mind. Recognizing the postman, Lamia opens the door wide.

"Ah, Ammar, there's my letter!"

The postman, his eyes riveted to Lamia's bosom, clears his throat.

"Hell . . . Hello, Miss Lamia! Yes, it's me! I've brought you your monthly registered letter from England. Some people have all the luck!"

Knowing how much he will enjoy it, Lamia gives a quick wiggle before she moves up close to him. She whispers in his ear, "Some others could have a bit of luck too if, with the letter, they would bring me a little bottle of Rive Gauche by Yves Saint-Laurent!"

The postman makes as if to caress the young woman's belly, then changes his mind.

"You think I can afford perfume on my lousy salary! Can I come in for five minutes?"

While continuing with her provocative hip swaying, the young woman takes the letter and pushes him away.

"Be good, Ammar! On the day of Aïd you'll be entitled to a little present . . ."

"But you know I won't be working that day!"

With a graceful, seductive movement Lamia glides into the apartment and closes the door. Alone on the landing, Ammar tries to get his breath back. His voice changes as if it had broken. It becomes guttural.

"She thinks she's going to spend her life turning me on. I'll have her . . . I'll have her . . . I hate women! I hate women!"

Disgusted, he spits on the ground, then climbs up to the next story while taking a small package from his bag.

"I hate women! Filthy lot!"

Boualem, bare-chested, his face half covered in shaving cream, razor in his hand, rushes toward the door before the postman batters it down. Ammar, out of breath and red-faced, holds out a parcel to him.

"Hi, Boualem! It's for you. Sign here."

Boualem is surprised.

"For me? Who could be sending me a parcel?"

"OK, I'll sign for you otherwise you'll mess up my book with your shaving cream."

Boualem takes the parcel and feels the weight of it in his hand. He tears off the wrapping paper. A piece of white cloth appears, as well as some soap and a small laurel branch. When he sees what is in the parcel the postman pales.

"God protect us! God protect us!"

"What is it ?"

Ammar lifts his eyes to heaven.

"A shroud!"

A worried expression flits across Boualem's face. Then he pulls himself together and smiles at the postman.

"I've already heard of this. These are the latest in anonymous messages. They send them instead of threatening letters. I'm being given a present of this soap and this shroud. How kind. I hope they'll also choose my grave for me."

Ammar has taken a handkerchief out of his pocket. He wipes his forehead.

"Don't joke about it. Someone's out to get you. Things are too complicated here just now. Better lie low for a bit. Keep quiet, don't go out, be better for you. Nothing but hate everywhere you look."

Boualem is still braving it out.

"Don't worry about it, Ammar. With the job I do, I don't have time to go out. Have a good day!"

The postman looks at him as if his days were numbered.

"My God! What's the world coming to? It's all the women's fault, all of this. I hate women! They're nothing but sluts, every last one of them!"

Boualem closes the door. He looks worried again as he goes toward the bathroom. Hanifa's voice makes him jump.

"Who was that?"

"The postman."

"Did he bring my alimony?"

Boualem doesn't answer. He quickly hides the parcel. Ammar runs down the stairs muttering his prayers. He doesn't even notice young Aïcha who is on the landing of the second floor. Looking like a ghost in her *hidjab* and her black headscarf, Aïcha is engulfed by the darkness at the end of the corridor. She stops still for a moment, waiting for the postman to disappear, then she knocks at the door.

Lynda opens the door, smiling.

"Hello, Aïcha! Finished your book already?"

"No!"

"So?"

"My parents are going back to their village tomorrow for the feast of Aïd. They're all going, with the children. For two days I'll be on my own."

Lynda smiles at her. She leans forward and whispers in her ear, "I hope there'll be no water cuts!"

Aïcha trembles. She feels her body go limp under her *hidjab*. She slowly takes a step backward while Lynda closes the door.

Back in the stairway once again, Aïcha sees Kader, Boualem's younger brother, carrying a large basket overflowing with vegetables. The teenager is happily whistling his Madonna song.

"Hello, Kader!"

He stops, puts down his heavy basket, and rubs his hand numbed by its handle.

"Hello, Aïcha!"

"Lucky I saw you just now! Could you buy me two packets of Marlboro?"

"Yes, but not right now. Sometime this afternoon, that OK?"

Aïcha takes a few coins from her pocket and gives them to Kader. He brandishes a packet of Dunhill's and takes out four cigarettes.

"In the meantime, I can lend you a few."

Aïcha's eyes open wide.

"Wow! Dunhill's! Wonderful! I adore them!"

Kader puffs out his chest and sniffs.

"Classy, eh? Not for any old body. Just taste that honey!"

Aïcha swiftly hides the cigarettes under her *hidjab*. She leans against the wall.

"How're you doing at the moment?"

"OK, OK. Slowly slowly. Planning my departure. Not long to the Toyota . . ."

"Did you get your passport?"

Embarrassed, Kader looks down.

"No, not yet! It's a bit complicated. But, by God, I'll get it before the end of the summer."

"Inch' Allah!"

Kader changes the subject. He starts ogling Aïcha's body.

"You know they're showing the latest Madonna film?"

Aïcha strokes his cheek.

"Oh yes?"

Kader blushes but doesn't give up. He tries flirtation.

"Yes, it's on at Houbel, if you're interested. I'm going to see it myself."

"Sure I'm interested . . . Perhaps we could go on the second day of Aïd."

"You're on."

Kader picks up his basket.

Aïcha returns to her apartment. As soon as she opens the door she is met by the screaming and shouting of the kids. "It's like a madhouse in here." And as the eldest she is responsible for the twelve kids, boys and girls borne by her child-laying mother, pregnant once again, in a small two-room flat "no bigger than a grave." For the moment Aïcha does not feel like refereeing the problems of the children fighting among themselves. She rushes into the toilet, locks herself in, and enjoys the luxury of smoking a Dunhill, deaf to the screams coming from the apartment. "It's true they taste like honey!" She smiles because she has just had a fleeting thought of her father working in the Bastos cigarette factory in Bab el-Oued who swore in his august position as head of the family that as long as he was alive no cigarette would ever enter his house.

KADER IS FOND OF Aïcha. "Yes, it's true, she does play around with her sexy *hidjab*, but she's nice all the same!" He's certain she's the only person in the block and in the neighborhood who understands him. At least, she listens and never contradicts him. And then she's the only girl he can take to the cinema. "We can go as far away as Houbel, the famous monument built by Chadli. Take two buses and you're in another world. If you've enough dosh you can buy yourself an ice cream. It's true they're pretty expensive! But I like to go and sit on the terrace with Aïcha because, despite her *hidjab*, she really turns the boys on, 'specially when she shows her knees and a bit of thigh . . ."

She's five years older than he, but for Kader that's just a detail of no importance, since she understands him. When they're together in the darkness of the cinema, she presses against him and caresses him. It's become a habit. "Nothing much! But it's great . . . The first time, I thought she hadn't done it on purpose. It was in a film . . . I can't remember its title, where they talked a lot about . . . you know what I mean . . . But as for the pictures . . . all the good scenes had been cut. Aïcha was not pleased. Her hand landed on my thigh and started wandering, so my rocket rose up . . ." Kader imagines the day when he will bring the Toyota back home. The wild outings with Aïcha. "OK, OK, the car's mainly for work, but it's important to have a good time too."

35

THE GREAT FEAST OF AÏD ARRIVED. THE RELIGIOUS FEAST OF THE sheep. That particular year, because of the violence in October and the mourning affecting some families, little ritual sacrifice was practiced. Usually the flocks of sheep were decimated. Families spent their savings to give their children the pleasure of leading around a sheep for a few days. The city vibrated with bleatings until the fateful day when the sheep's throats were slit.

The courtyards and terraces of the blocks of flats, the streets, and the public squares ran with rivers of blood. Children were grief-stricken as they watched their short-lived playmates put to death. But it was so exciting watching the animals writhing and the blood spurting out! And, at lunchtime, the dish of *bouzelouf* was much appreciated.

The day before the feast, Saïd, together with his group of beards, was responsible for ensuring that the area round the mosque was spotlessly clean. Imam Rabah knew by experience that there would be even more believers than usual at the main morning prayer on this holy day of Aïd than at the weekly prayers on Fridays. The surroundings must be in keeping with the importance of the event. Armed with brooms, washing powder, hose pipes, and bags, Saïd and the young volunteers worked hard to clean up until very late at night. "They can even eat off the pavement now, if they want!" Imam Rabah, a great advocate of cleanliness, was satisfied. And he felt it was much more beneficial to put Saïd's energy to use in this kind of action than anything else.

For Boualem the week of Aïd meant above all a harder working week. The black baking trays piled high with cakes were going to be shovelled into the oven one after the other. During this period of rejoicing and overeating families traditionally made their cakes at home. The women spent several evenings making them. Then the children came to the bakery with the baking trays filled with rows of cakes: *maqrouts*, gazelle's horn, *mantekaos*. There was constant coming and going and a permanent crowd in the shop. The oven was firing at full blast and Hassan, Boualem, and Mabrouk were exhausted by this extra duty which lasted until the eve of Aïd. Luckily the next day the shop would remain closed.

YAMINA IS WEARING a new skirt and blouse under her *hidjab*. She also has on a pair of Italian shoes bought in the *trabendo* market. With her mother she goes to the mosque where they take part in the main prayer of the morning before going to the cemetery to pay their respects, as is the custom, to the dead in the family. The security forces around the mosque are irreproachable. Rashid-Peshawar, prouder than ever, takes charge like a born leader, which does not prevent him from discreetly watching out for Yamina, "the bitch he adores." When she finally does appear, accompanied by her mother, Rashid bows and scrapes and shows them the way, which they know by heart, to that part of the mosque reserved for the women. Yamina doesn't even look at him. Lalla

Jamila gives him a quick smile to thank him for his help, though she does comment, sniffing delicately, "You'd think he might wash his clothes occasionally!"

"Who d'you mean?"

Yamina would like things to be over quickly. She can't stand the suffocating heat of the mosque despite the four fans that are on full blast. She can't stand the bodies packed so closely together, the stale smell of sweat, the nylon of the *hidjabs,* mixed with musk and bad perfume. What she really can't stand, though, are the hypocritical glances of the women and their idiotic whisperings. She knows that several girls are crazy about Imam Rabah and that one of them even has a photo of the preacher, which she has photocopied and secretly given out to her friends.

Yamina wishes she was already at El Kettar cemetery. Boualem's parents' grave is right next to her father's. She hopes to catch a glimpse of her beloved. El Kettar is such a beautiful place, so peaceful. Yamina loves to wander through the cemetery, to smell the perfume of the begonias, to read the names on the gravestones. She is, however, shocked by how much damage has been done. For some years now, the desecration of cemeteries has become almost current practice. Almost normal. The tombstones are systematically defaced with hammers by persons unknown who consider, for obscure reasons, that a dead Muslim has no need of decorations on his tomb and that a simple slab of cement or a few stones are enough.

The loudspeakers begin to broadcast the Aïd prayer throughout the neighborhood. Aïcha is happy. She did not bother to put on her *hidjab* this morning and wanders around the empty apartment wearing a large shirt, a cigarette hanging from her lips, impatient for Lynda to arrive. Her parents are in Barika, a small town high up in the mountains, far from Algiers. She knows that at this moment her father must be in the local mosque. After the main prayer he will go to sacrifice a sheep. The kids, enjoying themselves, are certainly roaming round the fields trying to ride the donkeys or kick the chickens. As for her mother, she must be in the kitchen as usual, among the women, slaving over the hot kitchen stove to prepare the feast-day meal.

And she, Aïcha, is here, in Bab el-Oued, alone and free! How lighthearted she feels! She is free to do absolutely anything she wants. For example, put the radio on full blast, walk around naked, smoke an entire pack of cigarettes, flirt with Lynda, go to the cinema the following day with Kader. She is preparing to flout these taboos in the space of one day without the slightest hesitation.

She knows Lynda has gone to visit the cemetery. She will be coming to join her as soon as she gets back. When she arrives, hot and perspiring, Aïcha will take her directly to the kitchen. The tubs full of water are ready and waiting. Aïcha will undress her, then start by raising her arms and gently soaping underneath them. She loves armpits. Especially when they have not been shaved. Ever since the two young girls started their secret games, Lynda has stopped shaving her armpits to please Aïcha. Afterward Aïcha will pour warm water over her entire body. Then cold water, making Lynda gasp. Aïcha will quieten her by kissing her, then will pour warm water over her own body. She has made life simpler by wearing a tunic which is easy to remove. Once their two bodies are wet, she will nuzzle up to Lynda, caress her, and continue to do so all day long. She knows she will reach orgasm several times today.

Aïcha's eyes close, her mouth goes dry and her skin damp at the mere idea. A ray of sunshine streams through the window and onto the rug. Aïcha stubs out her cigarette and puts on the radio which is broadcasting Andalousian music. She gets undressed and stretches out naked on the rug from the Aurès mountains, exposing her body to the hot rays of the sun.

Saïd had done a good job organizing the prayers at the mosque. "No problem." No pushing and shoving. A sermon from Imam Rabah, blunt and to the point, against speculators who, in this holy period, are doubling and tripling the price of sheep and giving them salted water to drink so as to increase their weight. The faithful naturally agree with the Imam's diatribes, but in their heart of hearts they know that "business is business." After the prayers are over, people embrace, wishing one another happiness and prosperity. Then they quickly disperse.

Saïd gets a lift in a friend's car to go and pray on his father's grave, recite a few verses of the Koran, and meet a few volunteers in charge of patrolling the cemetery. He lingers a little in the neighborhood, then goes home to lunch. In his family they had not killed a sheep. Lalla Jamila had prepared a couscous with red sauce, which Saïd loves. He had added a good portion of *harissa* and now bounds down the stairs of the block of flats. He does not see the shadowy figure lying in wait for him, hidden in a recess of the landing, who suddenly leaps out at him. Boualem grabs hold of him and won't let him go. Without raising his voice, but very firmly, he says, "You've been looking for me?"

Saïd can hardly breathe because of Boualem's tight grip. He whispers hoarsely, "We'll get you! We'll get you! You'll be sorry you were born."

Boualem shakes him violently.

"Choose your day! We'll settle it then."

Saïd wriggles free.

"I don't want any trouble right now, but don't worry, it'll be soon . . ."

"Whenever you want and that'll be the end of it."

Saïd's eyes are suffused with hatred.

"Goddamn you!"

Smiling slightly, Boualem watches him as he runs down the steps.

The animosity between Saïd and Boualem is almost as long-standing as Boualem's love for Yamina. They grew up in the same neighborhood, in the same block of flats, went to the same primary school, got involved in the same escapades. Saïd and Boualem, who were friends as children, were initially inseparable. They were quite different in character but they enjoyed one another's company, had the same problems as most other young people in the neighborhood and the country: *hogra*, the lack of any prospects for the future. As teenagers they spent a lot of time talking and planning to leave. They wanted to get some money together to escape from this country where they felt worthless: "a country where no one cares about us." Young men from Bab el-Oued, just like any others, finding their day-to-day existence rather tedious, with no specific goals, no hope of a future of any kind, who can only buy new clothes once their old ones are really worn out.

Their friendship lasted until Saïd noticed that Boualem rather fancied his sister. He felt this was an unforgivable betrayal. Once he got over the initial shock, he said nothing, but, as far as he was concerned, Boualem no longer existed. He found some footling excuse, some disagreement over a minor problem, to stop talking to him. Boualem never knew how Saïd had found out. That was the time when he would slip up to the terrace at night to see Yamina. He was very careful, yet nonetheless . . . As a result Yamina was forced to wear the *hidjab* and forbidden to go out alone. And there was absolutely no question of her going out to work. The silent animosity between the two boys continued to grow for years. When Boualem came across Saïd in the block of flats, in the street, in the mosque, they did not speak to one another, didn't even say hello. That was what the *redjla* of Bab el-Oued was like. And it could last a long time, even until death.

36

O N THIS SECOND DAY OF AÏD, HANIFA IS WORKING HARD IN THE TINY kitchen. She is preparing the leg of lamb that the uncle from Belcourt—who has sacrificed two sheep—has brought them. The uncle with a large mustache and potbelly comes to visit them with his children every Aïd to give them their share of the sacrifice: a custom whereby, on this holy day, the wealthier make a gift to a poor person they know, to be cleansed from their sins.

Boualem always arranges to be out when his uncle calls, since he can't stand him. "A big-headed shit stinking of his ill-gotten gains." For many years the uncle had been in charge of a *mouhafada* of the Party, a kind of local structure of the FLN in a small town of the Mitidja region, and both he and his wealth became visibly inflated. Contrary to other apparatchiks who acted with great discretion concerning their lifestyle, he unashamedly flaunted his wealth. He had his own philosophy, which he bluntly expressed: "In this country when people see power and wealth they have respect for you. They fear you and do what you want, which gets you even more money. That's the way it is, and you'll soon see how right I was. Look at the others, I know them all, those who've been stealing, who've been smuggling ever since Independence. They're afraid people'll know they've got money. They build a house, surround it with high walls so no one can see. They think that people would lynch them if they knew. Believe me, they've got it wrong! And they're not even enjoying being alive. Whereas I really enjoy life, and if I end up in prison, at least I'll have had a good time! Loads of them take their loot and go off to Paris. Being stupid and mixed-up, they all open Moroccan restaurants. See what I mean? Not Algerian restaurants because they're afraid people will start asking questions. But their Moroccan cuisine is so bloody awful that . . ." When he started on his moralizing economics lectures you wouldn't dare contradict him or ask questions. That was the way it was. He was top dog.

Algeria belonged to him, and to those like him. To keep power in his hands and prepare for the future, he placed his own children one by one in strategic positions. The oldest in the army, the second in the police force, the third in customs. He had obliged the fourth to become a lawyer. You never know . . . The fifth son, Sadek, was considered the black sheep of the family. Without anyone really knowing why, he had revolutionary ideas and was an active militant in the youth organization. An impenitent anti-imperialist who stood up to his father and was a real headache. "I don't believe it! This can't be my son. He's a monster. What sort of freak have I brought into the world?"

At the beginning of his first year at university, young Sadek went to the world youth festival in Havana. This discovery of romantic Cuba at the end of the 1970s strengthened his Marxist beliefs. "How wonderful! This people mobilizing on a small island, standing up to the American giant. If only we could be like them . . ." He had brought back in his suitcase a bottle of rum, which he guarded jealously in his room. His father found it and smashed it as a punishment. "No alcohol in this house! If you're so fond of Fidel Castro you should have stayed over there!"

Fortunately for the father, who suffered from high blood pressure when annoyed, Sadek's political obsession did not last long. During a trip to the USSR he discovered a fly in the ointment. At midnight one night when he was hurrying across Red Square to admire Lenin's mausoleum, he was accosted by two girls, "comrades, pretty and very friendly." It was only an hour later, when spending all his travel allowance in a bar, that he understood they were a couple of Moscow prostitutes. Next day, he began observing Moscow with a critical eye, and began to realize that this "great homeland of socialism" was not really paradise on earth.

He came back to Algiers and refused to speak for a long time, which his family couldn't understand. He was thoroughly shaken. Hurt. Disenchanted. He left the youth organization without explanation and started to write bucolic poems. His father, satisfied with the way things were turning out, found him a job in a ministry. The Ministry of Culture. He became a devoted crossword puzzle enthusiast and a passionate reader of the obituaries, which filled a whole page of the only newspaper each day. He was so bored in that ministry!

His father had been really worried. "Yes indeed, I was really worried. But all's well that ends well! Soon I'll find him a position in the Ministry of Foreign Affairs. We'll manage to find him a job in an embassy somewhere! How about Bangkok? Lots of business to be done there . . . D'you think we have an embassy in Bangkok?"

37

HANIFA HAS PRESSED KADER INTO SERVICE, IN EXCHANGE FOR SOME pocket money to go to the cinema in the afternoon. He has to help his sister prepare a meal and especially to keep her company. Sitting at a formica table in the kitchen, he is halfheartedly peeling some potatoes. The twins are sitting on sheepskins on the floor and playing with cardboard boxes. Kader is sulking.

"I'm going to have to spend all day peeling these potatoes. And this knife doesn't peel right. And all for fifty dinars."

"You'll get your fifty dinars if you do the job properly. And, tell me, who are you going to the cinema with?"

"With my mates! Anyway, I'm thirteen years old now! I can do what I want."

Hanifa doesn't answer. Kader looks up at her, then says, being deliberately provocative, "I've had a talk with Boualem. He agrees I can leave next year."

Hanifa, who was just inserting a clove of garlic into the leg of lamb, stops in mid-action.

"What're you on about?"

"That's what I said. I talked to Boualem yesterday. He's going to help me leave. I shall stay five years in New Zealand, get some *tawil,* and then come back and build a house."

"Another of your preposterous plans . . ."

Kader isn't listening.

"I'll bring back a Toyota bus and transport passengers to the Moroccan border."

Hanifa doesn't know whether to laugh or cry. She knows almost all her brother's little schemes but this is by far the best.

"He'll drive me crazy, the idiot . . ."

Kader is annoyed. He pushes back a strand of hair and faces up to his sister.

"The idiots are those who haven't understood there's nothing to do here if you're poor. In any case no one's going to stop me leaving."

He angrily peels a potato and furiously flings it in the saucepan full of water, splashing his face. Hanifa looks at him. She is touched. She feels even more affection for Kader when he comes out with things like that. She always wonders where on earth he picks up these absurd ideas.

"You will take me and the twins along when you go for a drive in your Toyota, won't you?"

Kader looks at her closely, to see if she is having him on.

"Of course! On my days off. But no one else, especially not Boualem."

"Well, why not? After all, he is your brother."

"Yeah, but things can start off all right and you never know how they'll turn out. The Toyota, it's for work, see? Get it?"

Hanifa pretends to take him seriously.

"Yes, I think so. But why Morocco?"

Feeling flattered, Kader settles himself in his chair before launching into a scientific explanation of his project.

"Because people go to Oudja on shopping sprees. I've heard the taxis are raking it in. With a Toyota I can fit in fifteen at one go and then put their stuff on the roof. See? If we only do one trip a week we'll be making a profit after six months. Get the idea?"

"Yes, great! But don't let that stop you peeling the potatoes!"

38

THE TWO DAYS OF THE FEAST OF AÏD ENDED ON A GLOOMY NOTE, AS they did every year. Too much eating, visiting the family, drinking large quantities of coffee. People got rather bored and, in the end, regretted the waste of money. Now life has returned to normal once more. The freezers are full of the remains of the sheep. In a few, more farsighted families, the meat has been salted and put to dry. Some scattered cases of indigestion here and there, then a halfhearted return to work.

The main Bab el-Oued market is back to normal and teeming with people. Only the butchers' shops are deserted because of the orgy of meat-eating over the past few days. Hassan-the-baker holds out his basket to the vegetable seller who chooses some juicy peppers for him.

"Today I'm going to tell my Jidjigua to make me a good old *choukchouka* for supper."

Rashid, who has been trailing him discreetly for some time, goes up to Hassan. After greeting him politely, he says in a low voice, "Hey, baker, I need to see you for a few minutes."

Hassan is surprised, and says to himself, "Another oddball I don't like too much. He looks as if he never changes his clothes. And I can't imagine what he wants to see me for."

Rashid insists on carrying Hassan's basket and walks away with him. When they reach a quiet side street, Rashid starts the conversation.

"You've heard about the loudspeaker someone stole from the terrace?"

Hassan shrugs his shoulders. "Surely this little shit isn't going to waste my time talking about the loudspeaker!" he thinks.

"Yes, yes of course! Everyone knows about that."

"Did you know the snake-in-the-grass who committed this act against Islam is close to you?"

Hassan stops in his tracks, intrigued.

"What d'you mean?"

"I mean to say it's Boualem who did it. We have proof!"

"Boualem?"

Hassan is stunned. "Boualem? I don't believe it."

"Yes, your fucking employee!"

"But why would he have done it?"

Rashid is annoyed. He is fed up with the baker's questions. He has a message to get across to him. Full stop. He has better things to do with his time than waste it with this guy he loathes. He becomes more aggressive.

"That's irrelevant. We got together and made a decision. He's got to be kicked out of Bab el-Oued."

"Well, and what's that to do with me?"

"To start with you're going to have to fire him from your bakery."

"But he hasn't done anything to me!"

Rashid-Peshawar puts down the basket and looks at the baker as if he were dealing with an imbecile.

"You don't happen to think that if someone attacks Islam they're attacking you too?"

Seeing Rashid's determination, Hassan begins to feel somewhat uncomfortable.

"That's not what I mean."

"Times have changed. Today, if you aren't with us, you're against us. And with your past . . ."

"What d'you mean, young man?"

Rashid places a firm hand on the baker's shoulder and his long fingers grasp his shirt collar.

"What I mean is, when you sucked up to the French."

"What?"

"Yeah. Well, let's not spend hours discussing that. You've got to fire Boualem, and today, otherwise you won't dare walk around the streets of Bab el-Oued."

Certain he has unnerved the baker, Rashid lets him go and gives him the bonus of a little slap on the cheek.

"See you Friday . . . In the mosque! And bring along some money; we've noticed you've been a little mean with your donations recently. *Salaam a'leikoum!*"

With this Rashid turns on his heel and disappears, leaving Hassan upset, rooted to the pavement, his basket at his feet. "Fancy that little runt daring to speak to me like that! Besides, what would he know about my past? Me, sucking up to the French! That son-of-a-bitch! If he'd been through what I've been through he wouldn't be talking to me like that, the creep. He thinks he's frightened me?" Hassan suddenly realizes he's become hot and bothered. He's suffocating, whereas moments ago he was enjoying the coolness of the morning. A drop of sweat rolls between his eyebrows and down his nose. "Shit! How can they possibly know about my past? They're worse than cops! Surely Aami Mourad can't have told them? Anyway, what does Aami Mourad know about me? Nothing! Except what I happen to tell him . . ."

Hassan bends down to pick up his basket. All at once the few kilos of vegetables seem to weigh a ton. He is still perspiring. And now he is trembling uncontrollably. "For heaven's sake! That creep has really put the wind up me! I didn't realize it would be so easy. Just one little sentence. But I don't believe it; why on earth would Boualem pinch their loudspeaker? I'm not going to get into trouble because of him. They're all the same. Why don't they just settle their problems amongst themselves? I'm too old for this kind of thing. Heaven's sakes! Why is this basket so heavy?"

Hassan starts walking fast, then faster and faster so as to put as much distance as possible between himself and Rashid. He is almost certain that "the creep" is spying on him, hidden somewhere not very far away, rejoicing at the idea of having touched exactly the right raw nerve. His weakest point: his past. His youth. His memories. His most prized possession. New drops of sweat course down his forehead and blur his vision. Everything around him becomes hazy and so much the better, because this means he can escape from the present, fly away toward the crazy evenings of yesteryear when there was that fantastic atmosphere they're trying to make him pay for today.

Those were the days of the wild parties at Padovani's, when Dario Moreno, Jean-Claude Pascal, Dalida, les Compagnons de la Chanson, or Jacques Helian and his orchestra came along to play on the summer evenings at Alger la Blanche. Hassan-the-then-teddyboy, "before that little runt Rashid was even born," thanks to his talent for rock-'n-roll, the paso doble, and particularly the slow blues, was a dab hand at pulling the French birds, so beautiful, so tanned, so hot, and who were so good at giving and receiving pleasure . . .

Hassan happened to be living in Bab el-Oued because he was then an apprentice baker at the Flower of Bab el-Oued, which at that time belonged to Mr. Puig, a "nice guy who liked to play pétanque, liked fishing for sea urchins, drinking anisette, and Sidi Brahim!" Mr. Puig allowed him to sleep in a corner in the back of the bakery, as long as he didn't make a mess of it, and above all as long as he didn't "bring back fatimas to screw on his day off."

It was in the bakery, after finishing work, that Hassan-the-teddyboy put on his white linen suit, slicked down his hair cut like Sacha Distel's, shined his shoes, and went out to conquer the world at Padovani's, the casino on the corniche, or any other temples of nocturnal pleasure in Algiers. Places where he had the privilege of being accepted because he was considered "an Arab not like other Arabs, good-looking, well-behaved—who dances like an angel. Not like one of those who would stick a knife in your back."

Hassan did not bring back girls (who, it must be admitted, dropped like flies) into the bakery for a smooch. He had his secret gardens, but what he really liked was to "do his own thing" outside, at dawn, on the cold sand of the beach of the Bain de Chevaux, taking care not to be rudely awakened by the dustmen bringing along the donkeys from the Casbah to be washed. The girls adored roughing it with him. He was a bon vivant, discreet, a night bird despite his work, and so fantastically virile.

He liked all the fashionable singers though he never had enough money to buy one of the new portable gramophones. "My God! That evening George Brassens came to sing at the Majestic, what a great evening that was! We all kept shouting, 'Go on George, sing us the one about the whores!' I even tried to get my mustache to look like his but it didn't suit me so I pruned it to look like Clark Gable instead!" Hassan was considered part of the French settler community despite the growing tension. One day in 1958, perched on the back of his Maltese friend Momo's Vespa, wearing a tricolor flag round his neck like a scarf, he was present at a rally in the Forum, an event he carefully avoided talking about. "And I hope there are no photos of me lying about anywhere! I went along to the Forum just out of curiosity. Just to see de Gaulle. I didn't even understand what he meant by his 'Je vous ai compris,' because when it comes to politics . . . In any case, whatever anyone says, he's the one who gave us our Independence!"

Toward the end of 1961 he had an idyllic love affair with Carmela, a fabulous Spanish girl, the daughter of an anarchist refugee. Suddenly his smooching days were over, things became serious, and he nearly got married. Unfortunately his plans fell apart because of the new upheavals in Bab el-Oued ushered in by the emergence of the OAS. Their Delta Commandos started gunning down Arabs, without really taking the trouble to find out whether those they were shooting were "those Arabs not quite like the others, who danced like angels, etc."

Hassan started to feel anxious in a city at war with itself. He practically never emerged from the bakery, under the nominal protection of Mr. Puig, reciting *chahada* each time he heard the explosion of a *strounga*. This prison-like existence drove him barmy. The worst thing was that he could no longer see Carmela whose father was working with the OAS.

In the streets of the city there were daily horrors, the chaos of civil war. The neighborhoods were divided up into precise zones, which certain communities were not allowed into for any reason whatsoever. Any Muslim going into Bab el-Oued, for instance, was murdered without warning. Hassan could no longer stand this sordid accumulation of dead bodies nor the nights of bomb explosions. A man's life was worth nothing. Everything that had happened since 1954, the FLN attacks, the battle of Algiers, the *maquis*, the repression, all these things had not much affected him, whereas what was happening now in Bab el-Oued had ruined his atmosphere and was tormenting him day and night.

The day he found out that the commandos also attacked cleaning women, he decided to disappear from Bab el-Oued. "I'm fond of my mates in this neighborhood but I don't fancy ending up in the gutter with three bullets in my head and my face covered over with newspaper to hide the blood!" Mr. Puig could not stop him from leaving. He went with him to the bus, sobbing, "How can things have gotten so bad, Hassan? Our beautiful Algeria . . ." In the afternoon Hassan was back in his Kabylian village where most of the men had either joined the *maquis* a long time before, had died, or were languishing in the camps awaiting the inevitable announcement of Independence. When the cease-fire was proclaimed, an unexpected development took place. Surprisingly it was the cities that exploded into violence whereas the countryside began to quiet down once the fighting had stopped.

Though Hassan did not stay long, his time in the countryside was nonetheless very beneficial. First of all it meant his life was saved, and then he rediscovered a certain "atmosphere" thanks to his young cousin Jidjigua who joined him late at night under the fig trees to be consoled for the loss of her fiancé: "not in the same league as the nights in Bab el-Oued, but Jidjigua was certainly charming and sensual!" For Hassan the most important thing was that it gave him an opportunity to claim he had done a bit of *maquis.* He had even managed to collect, with the help of his militant cousins in *wilaya* 3, a piece of paper with a stamp, the *bayane*, stating he had been a liaison officer between Tizi Ouzou and Beni Yenni. "That had me covered! Especially since certain bigmouths in the autonomous zone, who were no more in the *maquis* than I was, were now laying down the law in Algiers."

Back in the capital, he was heartbroken when he realized that the beautiful Carmela had disappeared. Her father had died during the siege of Bab el-Oued and she had immediately boarded a boat to Alicante. "God is all powerful!" A few days later Hassan made the best deal of his life in buying up at the eleventh hour and for a song the Flower of Bab el-Oued. He bought the bakery just in time, because the distraught Mr. Puig, in a fit of pique, had already planted ten kilos of plastic explosive and was getting ready to blow up the bakery before going into exile. As a bonus Hassan was even allowed to purchase his boss's red sports car after he had taken him and his wife to the harbor for their one-way crossing. It was only to his wife that Hassan confessed he had cried that day. "Must be feeling emotional or something . . ."

So it was that the Flower of Bab el-Oued ended up in good hands and continued to provide bread, croissants, and pizzas. Hassan, like everyone else, became an independent Algerian. He danced wildly on 5 July 1962 at the Place des Martyrs, then at the Place des Trois Horloges, to celebrate the return of peace and freedom. A few months later he returned to Kabylia and asked for the hand of his cousin Jidjigua whom he brought back to Algiers, married, and immediately made pregnant.

He panicked once again when the fighters of the *wilayas* began engaging in a desperate and incomprehensible war. Hassan lacked the political knowledge to understand that these were the first power struggles of the clans. He took part in a huge popular demonstration and yelled out the slogan "Seven years of war: enough, enough, enough!" then witnessed the triumphal entry of the National Popular Army—this great army that no one in Algiers had ever seen. "Fucking hell! If I'd known they had all those weapons I'd have joined up," he said, however, without too much conviction.

In fact, what made his life a misery was seeing that while he had managed to acquire Mr. Puig's apartment, "those others from

Morocco or Tunisia are busy grabbing all the villas on the coast and in the smart districts, as well as the shops in prime locations, and what's more they're helping themselves to antiques and furniture in the name of the revolution. Some revolution!"

Later on Hassan got used to the new Algeria, handed in his French identity card, and became a nationalist and follower of Ben Bella. He liked H'mimed, the new President of the young Democratic Algerian People's Republic. "I can go along with him as long as they don't stick a management committee in my bakery!" He went to the major meetings at the Forum—which revived certain memories—to those populist rallies during which Ben Bella improvised his speeches "in favor of socialism and against the bourgeois who were going to be 'slimmed down in the hammams.'"

Teddyboy-Hassan volunteered to go and plant trees on the hills of the *arbatache* during the socialist reforestation campaigns. That way he could take discreet little naps while the others dug the holes. He even had some photos of that period. Naturally he put his name down to go and fight the Moroccans about some border problem. "Fortunately I arrived too late. The desert war was over, otherwise who knows if I'd have been shot in the arse for some problem I didn't even understand. A war with the Moroccans, how bloody stupid when I've never even set foot in that country."

On the morning of 19 June 1965 he learned what the term *coup d'état* meant. Thanks to General Salan he already knew what the word *putsch* meant. His vocabulary was growing at phenomenal speed. He was sad about H'mimed, betrayed by his cowardly friends who imprisoned him and seized power, then he forgot about it, as did everyone else, and became a *Boumédiennist*. Things became more serious. The arguments were different. He joined the peasant socialist party of the colonel with the hollow cheeks and the teeth like Jacques Brel, and tried to turn a blind eye to his stern gaze and his determination to industrialize Algeria. He never understood what "industrializing industry" really meant, but that didn't matter. There were so many brains thinking for him in the ministries that he didn't have to worry his head about it. He danced once again—one last time—during the great Pan African Festival but did not volunteer for the agricultural revolution because there was something about it that bothered him. "Taking land away from the peasants! Sounds daft to me! And what's more, I'm not too keen on the minister of agriculture. Don't like the shifty look on his face."

Hassan realized, from popular rumors, that those "hypocrites who make the wonderful revolutionary speeches" were quietly stashing away fortunes. That did not prevent him from adoring the never-ending speeches of Boumédienne, which he listened to on the television, a glass of tea in one hand and his little daughter Houria on his knee. Especially when he announced that the oil industry would be nationalized. That pleased Hassan no end. He was proud to be Algerian. "He's right! It's our oil! Even if we can't sell it, we'll drink it! Hey, d'you think it'd taste like wine?" Hassan truly believed that Boumédienne was soon going to get rid of all the corruption around him. Happiness was within reach! What a great country Algeria was!

It was a little later on that certain practical problems emerged. At the time when they started building the "villages of the agricultural revolution," Hassan's red convertible broke down. It was impossible to find spare parts for it. He repaired the car as best he could for a time and then abandoned it in some wasteland to those who stripped down cars. That day he spared a thought for Mr. Puig of whom he had had no news. Perhaps he was dead . . . Hassan started taking the trolley bus to go into the center of town or down to the beach. The buses were crammed full of people, more and more of them, as in the streets of Bab el-Oued, as at the beaches, as in the shops. The city was becoming overpopulated. It was suffocating. Daily life was getting more and more difficult. Hassan no longer felt like going out. Bit by bit his world narrowed down to his bakery, his family, and his clients. He was becoming disillusioned.

In 1973, one morning in August, the lift in his block of flats (the last one still working in Bab el-Oued) stopped functioning forever. A new era was beginning. From now on Hassan was forced to climb up the five flights of stairs to get home. Really hard going when he was carrying jerrycans of water because of the increasingly frequent water cuts.

Chadli became President, and Hassan adamantly refused to become his supporter. "No, there I draw the line! Had enough of all this bullshit! The years go by and I see no change. Things are worse now! We're going backward. All I want is for them to get off my back and to deliver my flour regularly!" He did, however, change his mind for a short period when he found the Anti-Poverty plan very appealing. He bought a new fridge and stove and even brought home a washing machine. With "a little help from his friends" who were working in the socialist state-owned companies, he managed to get on the list for a Fiat 128. He waited patiently for a year, and when he went along to the warehouse to take delivery of his vehicle, in his innocence he wanted to choose a white Fiat. The official responsible for sales flew into a rage and almost tore up his voucher. "You crazy or something? Just be satisfied with what you're given and stop bullshitting us so early in the morning! If everyone started choosing their car color, then where would we be? You should thank your lucky stars that the state is giving you a car at all!" Hassan didn't press the point. He blessed the state and drove back home, proud and happy with his new acquisition: a green Fiat 128. The color of hope. In the meantime, gruyère cheese, "red cheese," and bananas arrived in Algiers. Happiness once again. That was enough for him to find Chadli not bad at all. "What? What's the problem? Looks like Jeff Chandler. Handsome face . . . elegant . . . And he's learned how to speak on television! Stop being hypercritical! Can't you see he's modernizing Algeria, and what's more he wears nothing but Cerruti suits! Have you ever heard of Cerruti?"

This state of grace did not last. Hassan had to sell his Fiat because the cost of living was constantly rising. After that there was "that sleazy Houbel who builds for the rich, abandoning us to our own devices. There's plummeting oil prices, more and more mouths to feed, and all those kids hanging about in the streets!" Each time he saw the President appear on the television he showered him with insults; of course, he now no longer bought the only newspaper. "*El Moudjahid?* That lying newspaper? Full of deadly dull articles . . ." He began listening to a Moroccan radio station, Medi-1, just when the tension between Morocco and Algeria was at its height because of the Polisario. "They do criticize Algeria but they're telling the truth, not like our television and radio! And for a start, what've the Sahraouis got to do with us? Eh? We've always got to go sticking our nose into things that don't concern us. And they're quite capable, one of these days, of going to war with Morocco!" The politician he hated most was the head of the only political party, the bearded man nicknamed Barrabas, with his broken teeth and sarcastic smile. Hassan really loathed him. And he wasn't the only one. "If that crook is a socialist, then I'm a Dutch uncle!" This shift in Hassan's attitude happened gradually. At about the same rate as the pauperization of the city, and at exactly the same time as a certain play was enjoying a runaway success among those who still went to the theater. The play summed up the entire situation in its title: *The Boat Has Sunk.* Hassan did not go to any of the performances. He never went to the cinema let alone the theater. He was looking for a refuge where he could shelter his resentment. This he found in the mosques, which he started attending regularly as places where, despite the repression, despite the arrests of the Imams, the truth could still be found. There were strangers who spoke from the bottom of their hearts, frankly, and had the gift of instilling new hope, while elsewhere cases of corruption and theft were on the increase.

Yes, he could kiss good-bye to those days at Padovani's. There was a sewage works there now, and the corniche casino was being used as a parking lot for the road repair trucks. Carmela and anisette were forgotten or at least tucked away somewhere in a secret drawer in the hidden depths of his memory. The *pieds-noirs* had long since left, taking with them their "atmosphere"; they too were long forgotten, erased from the landscape. "Algiers is becoming like the Far East, like Bombay, Calcutta! People walk happily through the filth! And as for that man! Only six months ago he was a barefoot nonentity and now he's just bought the latest Mercedes!" Hassan's convertible was dead and the Fiat 128 had been sold off in the El Harrach market. The market of disillusion. "Anyway, the Fiats all had defective engines and they rusted too quickly, which is why they were being sold to Algerians in the first place. Bribes and more bribes, brother! That's the name of the game!"

The Zanussi fridge and the Arthur Martin cooker were also starting to rust and fall to pieces. It was a real nightmare to get hold of spare parts for the kneading machine and the oven. But worst of all, and this he really could not accept, was that school had transformed his children into "morons, idiots who can't even string two sentences together! I, Hassan, who didn't even finish primary school, am a hundred times more intelligent than they are! What on earth do they do in the classrooms? Spend their time wanking or what?"

39

OUARDYA IS STRETCHED OUT ON HER BED, CLUTCHING A BOTTLE OF wine. She seems slightly tipsy. A cigarette is drooping from the corner of her mouth. Boualem is sitting on the edge of the bed. His hand is caressing her hair. He has come to see her because he feels like talking. He has told her of his troubles. The little parcel containing the shroud. Ouardya does not seem surprised. She smiles sadly.

"If I had to count all the threatening letters I've received I'd have enough for a book. It frightened me to start with. You can't imagine what I felt when I received the first one. Then I got used to it." Boualem looks away discreetly as Ouardya puts the wine glass to her lips. The room, as usual, is darkened. When Ouardya shyly nestles up to him, Boualem trembles. He quickly grabs a cigarette and lights it. He watches the wisps of smoke rising toward the ceiling.

"You never told me why you landed in this awful neighborhood."

Ouardya fluffs up the pillow. She closes her eyes, revealing the dark circles under them.

"Some things aren't easy to tell."

"I don't understand how you can live like this without going out."

"Why should I go out? The children do my shopping for me. You bring me my wine and cigarettes. That's enough. Algiers is a city I no longer want to see. I think if I went out now I would go crazy."

She takes a long drink of wine, then stretches out her hand and grasps the bottle on the floor near the bed. She fills her glass once again. Boualem covertly watches her.

"How did you end up here?"

"Isn't it strange! Since we've known one another, this is the first time you've ever asked any questions." Ouardya flings back her head, bites her bottom lip, and thinks back.

"A long time ago when we were students we dreamed of many beautiful things, of the revolution, of promoting the Third World, of Marxism . . . We were young left-wing militants and all our energy was devoted to serving the people. The country was young. The student movement was powerful, we were romantic, and I was in love."

Ouardya lowers her eyes. She continues to speak in a dull voice as if what she is saying has nothing to do with her.

"He was an incredible guy, only interested in politics, he wanted to change society. He gathered a group around him; we were very militant. One day we were all arrested. I spent nine days in a cell, but then they released me thanks to my father."

Ouardya's eyes fill with tears.

"My lover wasn't that lucky. I only saw him once. They brought us face-to-face. They were accusing him of all sorts of things. He had been disfigured by torture. I sensed I would never see him again . . ."

Boualem is moved. He wipes away Ouardya's tears.

"He has disappeared. I don't even know how. No newspaper ever mentioned him. Who could ever discuss military security?

Which of us could dare insinuate that our leaders did just as they pleased? I was afraid, like everyone else. And when I got over my fear, I realized that something had been destroyed in me. Forever. I didn't want anything anymore. Only to sleep. Sleep. And then I discovered this . . ."

She indicates her glass of wine and drinks a mouthful. She gets up, puts out her cigarette in an ashtray, then slowly moves toward the window and draws back the curtain. Sunshine floods into the room. The sounds from the street seem louder. Ouardya stretches out on the bed close to Boualem. He hesitates, then takes her in his arms. She wipes away a last tear.

"My grandmother lived in this apartment. I came to live with her until she died. My father sent me money but we no longer saw one another. He thought I was crazy. He preferred me to live here rather than have the scandal of my going to an asylum. It was hard . . . And now, there's you. I'm gradually starting to feel alive again."

Boualem looks at her. A shaft of sunlight falls on her hair and face.

"You look more beautiful in the sunlight!"

Ouardya does not reply. She buries her head in Boualem's arms.

"Don't look at me, please!"

"You're not going to spend the rest of your life shut away?"

"Why not?"

"Well, I don't know. You can't live like that!"

Ouardya smiles.

"You're waxing philosophical!"

"Wouldn't you like me to take you out one day? We could go for a walk somewhere."

"Maybe, but I need time to get used to the idea first."

40

SAÏD'S FINGERS DIG INTO THE BLACK LEATHER OF THE SEAT. OUTSIDE the car, the countryside, artificially darkened by the tinted glass windows, rushes by at great speed. Saïd wonders why these two guys have invited him for a spin in their "fucking stupid BMW." As before, they contacted him and fixed a meeting point on the road to Sidi Bennour, then the older man invited him to climb into the car. No explanations or comments. Just an order.

They have been driving now for more than three quarters of an hour. The two men are locked in an oppressive, deliberate silence. Saïd too does not attempt conversation, making do with unspoken contempt. His eyes are glued to their well-shaven necks. The young fair-haired man has a fashionable short undercut, no doubt styled by a good hairdresser downtown. Saïd would like to slide his sharp knife along this too-white neck, just to see the effect of the blood spurting out. He smiles slightly at this fleeting bloody vision, which gives him pleasure. The older man has a coughing fit. With a weary gesture he takes a bottle of cough mixture from the glove compartment and swallows a mouthful straight from the bottle.

The BMW is now racing through the poorest and most overpopulated districts of the eastern suburbs. In this incredibly ugly neighborhood large shapeless villas are stuck right next to the shantytowns and to huge tower blocks with cracks in their concrete walls. This higgledy-piggledy housing arrangement has grown up over the years flouting the most elementary regulations and standards. Some houses have been built right in the bed of the dried-out wadi. The fair-haired man with the signet ring speeds obliviously through the neighborhood. He never slows down even when children try to cross the street. He seems to take a morbid pleasure in missing them by a whisker, no doubt believing that even if he did hit one by accident he wouldn't be risking very much.

A foul smell is given off by the stagnant pools of water in the wadi and whiffs of it reach the inside of the car. The young man quickly puts up the window. Saïd is getting bored with this. "What exactly do these two bastards want? Why don't they ask me to do anything? Why are we driving round like this? What the hell are we doing in this neighborhood with this heat and dust?" These are the questions he is halfheartedly trying to answer. He knows he needs to be patient. Just to hang on. Right from the very beginning of his strange relationship with these men he has been kept in a state of deliberately maintained uncertainty.

THE FIRST TIME he saw them was on 4 October 1988, at the beginning of the riots in Bab el-Oued. The men appeared suddenly without anyone knowing who they were or where they came from. They were wearing filthy clothes, were unshaven, looked just like everyone else; they joined in the general destruction and even became ringleaders, telling the others exactly which shops to loot and set alight. There was total chaos and it never occurred to Saïd to question the unusual presence of two strangers amongst them. For the next few days he often found himself next to the young fair-haired man who wore his hair long then, did not yet have his signet ring, and did not look down on Saïd as he did now. Saïd quite took to him. Together they broke down the doors of the local branch of the National Bank, removed the large safe, and set it down in the middle of the road. They attacked it ferociously for two hours, without success. Then they gave up and left the safe to the kids and went off elsewhere to fight against police reinforcements.

After the first days of violence, the two men disappeared, and Saïd forgot about them. He was arrested the day of the bloody Islamist march but was not held, as he liked to tell his friends, in a cell in the police station. He spent a few hours in a room with another fifty or so rioters who had been arrested in different neighborhoods. The policemen did not even speak to him, weren't interested in him. At nightfall he was sent for and his eyes were blindfolded. He was thrown unceremoniously into a car and driven outside the town, on bumpy roads.

The real nightmare began when he found himself in a cell. It was completely dark. The oppressive silence made him panicky. He felt he was being observed though he wasn't certain. He began to be obsessed by the idea of death. He wanted to scream with fright but couldn't. He opened his mouth and nothing came out. If he stayed there a minute longer, he was sure he would go mad. He stood up and began walking round in circles, faster and faster. He realized he was crying real tears and did not have the strength to utter a single word, nor to control the spasmodic sobs choking him. Saïd discovered he was claustrophobic. He had never before felt such dread, such deep-rooted fear.

When the cell door opened, after a few hours or days, Saïd was a total wreck. He was ready to do anything to bring his nightmare to an end. The two men who put on the light and came into the white-painted cell were none other than those two who had taken part in the riots. Saïd was so exhausted he wasn't even surprised. The fair-haired young man looked him up and down, smiled mockingly, and offered him a cigarette. The older man spoke kindly to him, like a father rebuking his child. They promised they would get him out. They merely asked him, after he did get out, to tell everyone when he got back to his neighborhood about the torture he was supposed to have suffered at the hands of the police. "That won't be too difficult since everyone naturally hates the cops and they're not too fussy about beating up young people anyway." Then they suggested to him the story about having had his balls crushed in the drawer—a form of torture that really had been practiced on others—and took him to the bathroom so he could clean himself up. Saïd, gaunt and haggard, wondered if he was still alive.

The two men blindfolded him and took him to a car. As the car drove along a road bordered by orange trees—he could smell their delicate scent—they explained what they wanted from him and there was no way he could refuse. "It's nothing! The riots are over. Things are going to change. The country's going to change. We chose you because you interest us. We'll be in touch!"

He heard nothing from them for more than a month, then he received instructions for the first meeting. The two men came in their midnight-blue BMW. Saïd was on time. The idea of not turning up never even crossed his mind. The time he had spent in the cell had broken his will. He would be afraid of these two men for the rest of his life. They had nothing special to say to him. It was just a friendly, informal meeting, "to see if everything was OK."

From then on, every fortnight, a meeting lasting a few minutes took place on the hill of Sidi Bennour. Saïd wondered why they were wasting their time with him and what exactly they wanted. But the obsessive fear instilled in him by his claustrophobic night in the dark cell destroyed any temptation to disobey. He was dominated by these two men for whom he felt an obscure mixture of feelings: hatred, curiosity, and perhaps love. In the course of many sleepless nights after his arrest he asked himself countless questions, trying to convince himself they were not policemen. "They're something else, but I don't know what . . . Men from the services, maybe!" What most surprised him was that they never asked him what he did or whom he knew.

THE BMW STOPS near some wasteland. The older man turns round and smiles at Saïd.

"Well! Here we are. We must leave you now."

Saïd frowns to express his surprise.

"What are you leaving me here for?"

The man has another coughing fit. He puts a handkerchief over his mouth and spits into it. He glances disdainfully at Saïd.

"Surely you don't want us to take you back to Bab el-Oued and drop you among your friends?"

Saïd understands there is no point in arguing. "Those two are madmen, they're sadists. And God, the Almighty, has made me fall into their hands." He opens the car door and gets out into the street. The older man gives him a little wave.

"Hey, Saïd, just behind that tower block over there, there's a lovely little mosque. It'll soon be time for the prayer."

Saïd glares at him, wondering whether he is being serious or sarcastic. The young fair-haired man impassively admires his signet ring. In a flash the BMW surges forward, leaving Saïd behind in a cloud of dust.

41

BOUALEM IS TRUDGING DOWN THE STREET LEADING TO THE HAYAT mosque. He has decided to go and talk to Imam Rabah since he is certain that Saïd is planning something against him. He knows Saïd too well to realize he won't give up, in his cunning way. Now that Saïd knows about the loudspeaker, and especially about his meeting Yamina in the church, the situation might get badly out of hand. Mabrouk has already had a serious beating up because of him. Things can only get worse. Imam Rabah's intervention and authority alone can put an end to this conflict.

Boualem is thoughtful. He has just emerged from Ouardya's bed and cannot quite understand why he made love to her. He enjoyed it, he must admit. She gave him a great deal of pleasure, but while he was in her arms, he couldn't stop thinking about Yamina. The ambiguity of his relationship with Ouardya is spoiling his life as much as the problems arising from his stupid act on the terrace. Boualem increasingly feels it is necessary for him to leave, to put a great distance between himself and Bab el-Oued, "this neighborhood that has become as black as tar between my eyes!"

IMAM RABAH RECEIVES HIM in the reading room. He seems worried, though pleased at Boualem's visit. "A nice boy, honest, uncomplicated. Not very active in the fight for Islam, but with time . . ." He speaks to him in a calm voice, trying to be soothing.

"You know, Boualem, as the days go by I feel we're in for troubled times. I don't know what to do. I try to talk about tolerance and I have the feeling young people aren't listening to me. Some people, I don't know why, are preaching *fitna*."

Boualem thinks Imam Rabah is also partly responsible for the oppressive atmosphere in Bab el-Oued, with his inflammatory sermons and the daily agitation around the mosque. But he is careful not to say so. What's the point? Especially since this man is gentleness itself. A gentleness that turns into dynamite when he climbs up to the *minbar* and becomes a preacher. Boualem thinks the Imam could have been a rocker if he had been living in another country. The thought makes him smile. The Imam does not notice. Boualem goes straight to the point. "Since last October Saïd has been acting like the leader here!"

"I know! I know! After he was arrested during the riots you all made a hero of him. In the stadiums, at assemblies . . . You put him on a pedestal."

"I don't deny he was brave, but now he wants to lay down the law."

"And you've just played into his hands through your childish gesture, Boualem. You'll have to put back the loudspeaker."

Boualem is barely surprised to find out that the Imam knows all about it.

"I threw it in the sea."

The Imam smiles.

"I like you, Boualem, because you are pure, direct. But you are really a child!"

Boualem hangs his head in embarrassment. The Imam gets up.

"This neighborhood is getting too much for me. Give me a few days and we'll calm things down."

"Oh, sheikh! He mustn't needle me too much or there's no knowing what I'll do . . ."

"Don't say such things in God's house! Come! Let us pray!"

The Imam leads Boualem into the prayer room. Ever since he found out about it, he has been puzzled by what Boualem did but does not ask any questions. Boualem seems to read his mind.

"I don't know what got into me. It all happened so fast, I couldn't control myself. It was probably because of the noise!"

"Do you really think it was the noise?"

"I don't know . . ."

"More likely to be the devil! Sometimes when he worms his way into our thoughts he is so sneaky, so deceitful that we can't resist. That's why some of our acts seem inexplicable."

"That must be it."

42

NIGHT IS SLOWLY FALLING IN BAB EL-OUED. THE TERRACES ARE swarming with women taking down their washing, folding it, and piling it up in baskets. Hanifa and her neighbors are in a hurry to finish their task because of the damp rapidly setting in.

Boualem went back to Ouardya after his interview with the Imam. He wanted her again. He didn't think about it. She too wanted him. This time he didn't think of Yamina and didn't feel at all guilty. They made love for a long time, in silence. Now, stretched out on the bed, he is smoking a cigarette and dozing. He is light-headed and feels good. At peace. Ouardya is beside him, hungry for words to fill her loneliness.

"I have this recurring nightmare. I am holding a baby in my arms and I let it fall. I can't do anything about it. I am paralyzed and then it comes back into my arms without my knowing how. And then again, it slips out and falls down into a black hole . . ."

Boualem is barely listening to what Ouardya is saying. This business of dreams and nightmares is too complicated for him. To tell the truth, he's afraid of them. His mother, when she was alive, was a specialist in the interpretation of dreams. For each image she glimpsed in her sleep, she would little by little unravel the threads that led her to interpret what she thought was the hidden message coming from the beyond. Boualem dared not talk to her of the images that disturbed his nights. Yet ever since his childhood he has never stopped having dreams, nightmares, leaping out of bed wet with perspiration as if he were trying to escape the flames of hell. But as soon as adolescence was upon him he decided he would stop telling his mother about the apparitions haunting his sleep. He could no longer stand her bringing in death, the ancestors, heaven, and hell.

Hanifa also knew how to interpret dreams. Of course she got this science of the occult from her mother, and claimed that since her mother's death she spoke with her once a week in her sleep. At the beginning she tried to tell her dream-dialogues to Boualem but, sensing his reluctance, she gave up.

BOUALEM FALLS ASLEEP while Ouardya is speaking, the ash still balanced on the end of his cigarette. Ouardya looks lovingly at him, strokes a strand of his hair, then wakes him up when she has made him a coffee.

43

DAZED AND DRY-MOUTHED, BOUALEM DIVES INTO THE BAKERY WHERE Mabrouk and Hassan are already at work. He greets them and takes off his denim jacket. He is just about to take off his vest.

"Don't bother to get undressed."

Hassan has spoken without raising his head and without looking at Boualem. His voice is strange, thick with emotion. Mabrouk doesn't raise his head either. He turns off the kneading machine and moves away. Hassan clears his throat. Boualem stops what he was doing and looks at his boss.

"What's up?"

"I . . . I don't know how to tell you but you can't stay with us any longer . . ."

Boualem smiles. "Is this a joke?"

He looks at Mabrouk who pretends to be engrossed in his chewing tobacco.

"No, it's serious. I've got real problems; I can't keep you any longer," continues Hassan in the same vein.

"Aren't you satisfied with my work?"

"It's not that! You know quite well what it's about. Come back tomorrow, I'll give you what I owe you. We'd better let things calm down for a while."

Boualem snatches up his jacket. His face is ashen.

"OK, I've got it. You're shit scared. You're all shit scared. There's lots of other bakeries in Algiers."

Boualem leaves the bakery without saying good-bye. Mabrouk puts the chewing quid in his mouth. Hassan violently throws a lump of dough into the kneading machine before yelling, "Shit! I'm not going to lose my business just because of him and his stupid games."

44

SIRENS SCREAMING, A POLICE CAR HURTLES UP THE CENTRAL AVENUE of Bab el-Oued, screeching to a halt in the Place des Trois Horloges. Near the smashed window of a pharmacy a small crowd of people are gathered round an ambulance and a body lying on the ground, covered by a sheet: the signs of a tragic incident at this late hour of the night. A police van is parked a little way off.

Inside are the crumpled figures of Tahar and Ali, the young junkies of Rocher Carré. Their faces are blank, their vacant stares indicative of their state. Standing next to an unmarked police car, an inspector is busy on the phone while his colleagues, who seem jittery, are trying to hold back the ever-increasing crowd.

"Yes, that's it, a holdup in a pharmacy. Stole some drugs. One dead from a massive overdose of barbiturates. We've got the other two. Youths from this neighborhood. Completely out of it! Must've popped a kilo of pills!"

The windows and balconies of the surrounding blocks of flats are crammed with curious onlookers, men and women, witnessing the spectacle of death. Boualem, wandering round the streets to dispel his anger, sees the crowd. He pushes his way through and is in the front row when an inspector uncovers the face of the body lying on the ground. The contorted face of Karim appears. Boualem recognizes him. He can't help retching. He turns away and leaves.

The inspector covers up the body and the ambulance men put it on a stretcher. The policemen try to disperse the crowd, which is growing all the time. Mainly young men. Some have come down from their homes in their pajamas, others are wearing the *qamis* or *gandoura*. Their voices are getting louder and louder, commentating, accusing, insulting one another. The tension rises perceptibly. A child goes up to Boualem and gives him a note.

"From Saïd!"

Boualem reads it, then throws it away. He looks for Saïd and his gang while accusations are zipping back and forth through the crowd.

"Just look what you've done to us!"

"We're fed up with this *hogra!*"

"Are you going to kill us all?"

"We want an Islamic state!"

"Death to thieves, death to corruption!"

"We're martyrs here in Bab el-Oued!"

The police inspector changes tack in his telephone conversation, speaking in a low voice while checking his revolver under his arm.

"Things are getting out of hand here. Better send reinforcements immediately, we may be in for trouble."

Suddenly, from nowhere, a large stone smashes the windscreen of the police van. Boualem walks off. Feeling sad and aimless, he continues to wander through the deserted streets among the cats and piles of rubbish. The noise coming from the area around the Place des Trois Horloges gets louder and louder and is then suddenly punctuated by several muffled shots. Shrieks are heard. Then police or ambulance sirens, followed by silence.

SITTING IN THE DARKNESS of his room, Boualem stubs out his cigarette and gets up. Without making any noise, he takes the keys of the terrace hanging in the hall, leaves the apartment, and climbs up to the roof. He settles in a corner of the terrace and sobs as he smokes a cigarette. He doesn't really know whether he is grieving for Karim, who has just died like a dog in the street, or for his own fate. Unable to find an answer to help him forget his anger, he sniffles like a child, wipes his eyes, and goes toward the parapet opposite Yamina's window. A feeble light is burning there. Boualem takes a box of matches from his pocket. He lights one and holds it in his finger until it burns down, then lights a second, then a third. As he used to during their secret meetings. That was how he let Yamina know he was on the terrace, at night, when everyone was asleep. The wavering flame lights up the young man's face. Tonight Yamina does not appear at the window. Boualem gets up and leaves the terrace.

His thoughts return to Saïd and to the note that he was given in the street. "Since the bastard wants things settled tonight, let's have it out tonight!"

45

A FULL MOON IS SHINING DOWN ON ROCHER CARRÉ, CREATING A DREAM-like décor to which the lapping sound of the water adds a slightly scary note. Boualem climbs over the rocks towards the massive concrete block projecting into the sea. He trips, picks himself up, continues walking. Once he gets to the top of the block, he spends some time looking at the huge, threatening, black waves smashing into the rocks, then quickly gets undressed.

He dives in straightaway. His body disappears in a fraction of a second, swallowed up by the waves. Holding his breath, he tries to swim underwater as long as he can. With a few powerful strokes he sinks into the silence of the cold liquid night. A feeling of peace, sensuousness, and calm steals over him.

He has always loved swimming underwater ever since he was a child. As a teenager he always tried to dive down as deep as possible, never wanting to use a mask or snorkel. He liked to be alone under the water for a long time. He would close his eyes and stretch himself to the limit.

Tonight Boualem feels he is pushing himself too hard: his lungs are at bursting point. He propels himself to the surface with a swift kick. He swims unhurriedly, gradually resuming his normal breathing pattern as he returns to shore. Dripping wet, he climbs up onto the rocks, picks up his T-shirt, dries himself with it, puts on his trousers. Feeling calmer now, he smiles and takes his pack of cigarettes out of his pocket.

Just as he is lighting up he sees in the distance some figures outlined against the rocks: Saïd and his friends are approaching. Rashid is the first to catch sight of Boualem, and he signals to his companions. Boualem soon recognizes them. He stands up and waits, a mocking smile on his lips. The group speeds up and quickly surrounds Boualem, who does not attempt to escape, who is ready for confrontation: that is why he has come. He has followed Saïd's instructions.

When the kid gave him the note Boualem couldn't help having a fleeting feeling of affection for Saïd. "He wants a duel on the rocks, like in the American films. *Rio Bravo, OK Corral . . .*" He knew Saïd loved all that. The action . . . The spectators applauding . . . Boualem agreed to play the game. His swim has just tightened his muscles. He feels ready.

"Shall we settle it *rass rass* or do you need them?"

Saïd doesn't answer. He merely gives him a sardonic, disdainful smile, dismissing the question. He signals imperiously to his friends to stay behind while he continues to advance toward Boualem. For greater freedom of movement he is not wearing his *qamis*.

Suddenly things speed up. Without a single word being spoken a violent, merciless fight breaks out. The sound of the waves covers that of the blows. Boualem, lithe and agile, defends himself well. Saïd, heavier and fitter, hits out with several violent blows. He enjoys punching, causing pain. If they had been alone he would have yelled out his fury at Boualem for having dared get close to his sister. He would shower him with insults, the nastiest, the filthiest. But now, with the others there, his resentment is concentrated in the strength of his punches, which are saying it all for him. Boualem defends himself and counterattacks. After a few moments he has the upper hand over Saïd, who receives a series of well-calculated blows, which bloody his face.

At the age of about sixteen, like many other young lads from the poorer neighborhoods, they became interested in boxing. For a year Boualem assiduously attended a training course in a cellar somewhere in Climat de France. He closely followed the advice of

Ghoumri, the ex–regional champion, an excellent trainer, who became half crazy after his only fight in Tunisia, whereas Saïd only flitted in and out, more interested in his afternoons in the bars. Today he is paying the price for not having taken it seriously.

Suddenly he stumbles and falls to his knees, stunned by Boualem's direct punches and uppercuts. Worried by the way the fight is going, Rashid, then his friends, intervene. Only Mess holds back. Boualem hits two of the attackers and knocks them off balance but he is quickly outnumbered. Saïd, completely groggy, moves aside to try to get his breath back. A few meters away the beating up starts.

Rashid, beside himself with fury, lays into Boualem who is already unconscious. "I'm going to finish him off, there'll be nothing left of the filthy bastard!"

"Stop! That's enough!"

Despite the blood flowing from his mouth, Saïd is almost pleading with them because he senses that Rashid is muscling in on his act. He wants to get some strength back and continue to fight. Rashid is past hearing. Boualem is also *his* enemy. He's not going to miss this opportunity.

"I'll wipe him out, the filthy swine."

Mess leaps at Rashid and tries to restrain him. Two of the bearded followers pick up Saïd and help him to his feet.

"Steady now. Leave him alone. Can't you see he's had enough? Calm down. Time to go."

Mess pulls off Rashid who offers no resistance. The group goes away, leaving Boualem unconscious on the rocks.

46

BEHIND HIS COUNTER AS USUAL, HASSAN IS HUMMING AN OLD ALGIERS tune, but this morning his heart isn't in it. He can't understand how he can have behaved so despicably toward Boualem. Just one little sentence from Rashid-Peshawar and he feebly obeyed his orders. Was it fear? Submission? He can't understand. Mabrouk hasn't spoken to him all night long. His view is that, after all, Hassan is the boss and has the right to run his business as he likes. But one thing is sure: he will have to give up his job out of solidarity with his mate. After having a wash he is getting ready to leave the shop, with six loaves under his arm, listening to his new Walkman. Hassan knows he's sulking. Irritated, he shouts to Mabrouk, "If you see Boualem, tell him not to forget to come and collect his money this afternoon."

Mabrouk has heard despite the earphones but leaves the shop without answering. He is not interested in what Hassan said. He doesn't even want to look at him. "We spent all that time working for this creep!"

When Mabrouk has left, Hassan lets his anger explode. "Don't bother to pretend you didn't hear! I can do without you, too! And I can even, if I want, close this rotten bakery and get out of this fucking neighborhood and leave this city of crooks. I've still got my place in Kabylia. I won't have to see all your fucking faces anymore!"

An early morning customer, coming into the shop, looks at him in surprise, wondering whom he is speaking to. Hassan vents his anger on him. "And what the hell do you want, so early in the morning?"

"What? Me? Nothing, nothing . . ."

"That's just as well, because if it's bread you want, you can stuff it up your arse!"

The client flinches, backs off, and leaves the shop.

47

LIKE EVERY OTHER DAY SINCE THEY CAME TO ALGIERS, PAULO AND HIS aunt have set off early on their walk: they like to enjoy the coolness of the morning. A taxi dropped them at the gray stone esplanade, right next to the large Rocher Carré. Paulo's description of the scenery to his aunt becomes more and more beautiful and more and more unreal. Right from the beginning of her stay the old lady has not been taken in by what Paulo has been telling her, but she goes along with it, like a child listening to a fairy story.

"Padovani Beach hasn't changed. If only you could see all the multicolored parasols, then there's the pedal boats, d'you remember the pedal boats?"

"Yes! But there were also the sewers at Bain de Chevaux."

Paulo smiles. Right in front of him the sewers are emptying their outflow onto the sands.

"No, no, there aren't any more sewers. Everything is spotless. There can't possibly be any sewers here, since people are swimming. And behind there is El Kettani, just next to Padovani. It's become a complex. You'd think it was Miami Beach. I don't see why tourists would go anywhere else! Here's where it's at. If the water were warm, I'd love to go in."

The aunt sarcastically raises her walking stick. "This used to be the helicopter landing pad in the old days."

Paulo looks carefully.

"I can't see it. Was that during the war?"

All at once he sees a shape lying between two rocks, just a few meters off. He looks away and takes his aunt by the shoulder.

"Well, Auntie, it's time to go to the cemetery now . . ."

BOUALEM IS STILL LYING half unconscious on the rocks. The blood has clotted on his face. He gradually regains consciousness, opens first one eye, then the other. His face twists with pain. He gets slowly to his feet and makes a superhuman effort to stay upright. He staggers about, still dazed from the blows he has received.

48

THE TERRACE OF 13 RAMDANE-KAHLOUCHE STREET IS BUSTLING with activity. Saïd is busy, helped by his friends. The women have been told they must leave the terrace for an hour. Saïd is satisfied and even in good spirits, despite the many bruises on his face, a reminder of the fight. He has hardly slept at all. After dressing his wounds he went to the mosque for the morning prayer. He was surprised to find the parcel already there. The loudspeaker ordered by the Imam had arrived. It had reached the port of Annaba and a militant had delivered it right to Algiers. Imam Rabah, looking at Saïd's wounds, immediately understood what had happened and did not ask any questions.

After setting up the brand-new loudspeaker, Saïd smoothes his beard and taps his faithful follower Rashid on the shoulder.

"What a beauty! Latest Italian model, even more powerful than the last one. I don't think any other son-of-a-bitch'll feel like removing it."

Rashid starts, offended by Saïd's vulgarity.

"Here, Saïd, watch your language! What if the Imam heard you!"

Saïd laughs. "I don't give a shit about the Imam. One day I'll be the Imam here."

He looks disdainfully at the satellite dishes scattered round the terraces.

"And when that day comes, we'll do something about these crappy satellite dishes: smash them to pieces with hammers."

49

B OUALEM STAGGERS ALONG THE MAIN AVENUE CROSSING BAB EL-OUED. As always in the early morning the streets are full of people, some in a hurry and others idly ambling along. Boualem's blood-streaked face attracts people's attention and provokes some comments from the passersby. "They're a rough lot round here . . . winos beating each other up." All Boualem can hear is a fierce buzzing in his head. He walks like an automaton, looking straight ahead.

So as not to frighten his sister, he goes to Ouardya first of all. She opens the door and shrieks with fright when she sees the state he is in.

"My God!"

The exhausted Boualem goes into the sitting room.

"Don't worry, it isn't serious . . ."

"Lie down, I'm going to clean you up."

He collapses on the bed and can't help groaning with pain. The blood has started flowing again. His eyebrow is split. Ouardya returns very quickly. She cleans the wound, which makes him yelp again.

"Was it Saïd?"

"Yes! And his pals . . ."

"They're dangerous. And the whole neighborhood is behind them."

"You say that too!"

"I don't want to lose you! I'm going to leave here. You could come with me. I've got some money . . ."

Boualem looks at her tenderly. He doesn't answer. His bones are aching. The night he spent on the rocks, the blows, the bath have all been too much. Everything becomes blurred. He passes out.

50

A NOTHER WEEK IS DRAWING TO A CLOSE, JUST LIKE ALL THE OTHERS, in a city where the predominant feeling is one of boredom. Like every Friday, the great hall of the mosque is full of the faithful. Imam Rabah, high up on his *minbar*, is beginning the second part of his sermon, his voice choking with emotion.

"In the name of God, the merciful, the compassionate . . . Let us continue. I have been informed of acts of violence which took place the other night on the rocks. I think things are now clear.

There are some amongst us, fellow Muslims, who do not want peace in this neighborhood. There are some amongst us, fellow Muslims, our own children, who want *fitna . . .*"

In the hall, Saïd, sitting on his mat, looking blank, meets the gaze of the Imam. He attaches no importance to what the preacher is saying. He is quite confident that the situation is developing as it should. To his advantage. Now the whole neighborhood knows who was responsible for the theft of the loudspeaker and that the culprit has been suitably punished. Saïd has been congratulated by the young men and is pleased with himself for what he did and the resulting consolidation of his authority. The conciliatory words of the Imam are not going to change anything at all.

However, what Saïd does find puzzling is the presence, at the back of the mosque, of the mysterious fair-haired man with the signet ring. For some time now he has been present for all the prayers. Imam Rabah continues to stare at Saïd.

"Violence begets violence. And Bab el-Oued, our neighborhood, will never find peace. Is that what our children want? At the moment we are ready to kill one another, for trivialities. Amongst our neighbors. Fellow Muslims. Is that what the Holy Koran teaches us? In truth, I believe this neighborhood will never be at peace again, and I have decided not to remain here where hatred has taken root. My friends, I must tell you I have made up my mind. My moral authority is worthless now. So I am leaving. I shall go to a region where hearts are still pure."

Saïd lowers his head. A murmur runs through the hall. Harsh looks are turned on the young man. Saïd did not imagine the Imam would dare to publicly disavow his action in this way. He gets up and leaves the mosque while Imam Rabah continues with his sermon.

"I am not leaving to escape. I am leaving so that my act will be a warning. So that you will know, my brothers, that you are responsible for what happens to you and that you will only have yourselves to blame. May salvation be with you."

With a catch still in his voice, Imam Rabah recites a sura from the Koran.

51

THE LARGE MIDNIGHT-BLUE BMW APPEARS AT THE TOP OF SIDI Bennour hill. Saïd, standing near the parapet, nervously smoothes his beard and goes up to the car when it stops. The fair-haired man with the mustache and the signet ring gets out and walks toward the wall, completely ignoring Saïd. He admires the view. The older man, still in the car, starts to speak in his slow commanding voice.

"Hello, Saïd! This time, we haven't made you come for nothing!"

Saïd, suddenly annoyed, points at the fair-haired man who has moved away.

"I'd like to know what he's doing spending his time in the mosque. He's spying on me, isn't he?"

"Calm down! You're not going to prevent people praying if they want to, are you?"

"I don't get it and I don't like it."

"Listen, you, we're not here to chat about the weather. Serious things are going to be happening soon and I have brought a little present for you."

The man holds out to Saïd an object wrapped up in a thick cloth. When he takes hold of it Saïd's angry outburst disappears as if by magic, giving way to fear. Feverishly he removes the cloth and uncovers a gun, a large-caliber revolver. Apparently unruffled he weighs the revolver in his hand, then throws a surly look at the man who now gives him two little boxes.

"Cartridges. Don't fool about with the gun while waiting for the next contact. It's valuable. Hide it somewhere at home and forget about it."

The fair-haired man has returned. He sits down at the wheel and slams the door. He speaks to his friend.

"I could spend all day here looking at the view. When you think there are some idiots who want to destroy this city . . ."

He suddenly revs up and the car skids and surges forward. Saïd just manages to leap backward in time to avoid being run over. The BMW disappears. He wraps the revolver up in its cloth and slips it into the pocket of his jacket, then remains at the edge of the road, not quite knowing what to do. All at once he bursts into tears and sobs like a child.

52

A FIGURE CLIMBS SWIFTLY AND STEALTHILY UP THE DARK STAIRWAY. AT the last story, on the landing leading to the terrace, Yamina stops. She holds her breath and listens. A noise makes her jump. She looks up and sees the shadowy outline of Boualem waiting for her, crouching near the door to the terrace.

"Don't be frightened! It's me."

"I'm afraid we'll be seen . . ."

"I've got the keys. We can go onto the terrace."

"No! No! I can't stay long."

"I've got to talk to you!"

Yamina moves closer to him.

"I know what Saïd did to you. I've also suffered from his brutality. He's out of control. I don't know what's happening to him."

"Forget that. What I wanted to say was, I've . . . I've decided to leave."

Yamina impulsively leaps into his arms. Boualem hugs her to him.

"Leaving? Where'll you go?"

"I don't know . . . The world's a big place. I've got contacts."

"And what about me?"

"I'll come back for you."

Yamina's eyes fill with tears.

"I know I'll never see you again. You'll disappear like all the others who go away . . ."

"No! I swear I'll come back for you. I love you!"

Boualem gently wipes away the tears and caresses Yamina's eyes. They draw closer together. Their mouths meet for the first time. Boualem murmurs, "If Saïd wasn't your brother, he'd be dead by now . . ."

"Don't say that."

"Don't worry about me. That's forgotten already. I've put it behind me. I love you! I'll come back for you . . ."

53

OUARDYA, WOKEN UP BY SOMEONE HAMMERING ON HER DOOR, GETS out of bed and opens up, thinking it must be Boualem come to visit her. Saïd brutally grabs hold of her and pushes her into the flat. Brandishing the large revolver, he hurls her against the wall and screams in her ear, "Enough of this fooling around! You've got one week to get out! Enough of this filth, this drinking . . . Enough of this bad example to the children . . ."

Ouardya is paralyzed by fear.

"One week! Got that? Or you'll get three bullets in your head."

Wild-eyed he glares at her, then puts the barrel of the revolver against her head and pulls the trigger. The click of the hammer against the empty chamber makes Ouardya shudder. She closes her eyes. Saïd guffaws, "Next time, there'll be bullets!"

He lets go of her. Still propped against the wall, Ouardya starts shaking uncontrollably.

"You're shit scared, aren't you, slut!"

He turns away and goes into the sitting room, which he begins inspecting.

"Is this your brothel? It stinks of wine and sperm!"

He goes into the kitchen and discovers a dozen wine bottles on the table. He sweeps them off with his arm. They fall and smash on the floor in a crash that can be heard throughout the block of flats. Saïd returns to Ouardya, his eyes glittering with pleasure. The young woman has not moved. Petrified, she hasn't realized what is going on around her. Saïd stops, looks her up and down, then sticks the gun barrel into her belly. Ouardya is too distraught to react. Embarrassed by his gesture, Saïd murmurs a prayer and rushes out of the apartment, slamming the door.

54

MABROUK APPEARS AT ONE END OF THE LONG PASSAGEWAY TO THE harbor. Wearing a black Public Enemy cap on his head and carrying two large plastic bags full of cheap new goods, he walks quickly, eager to get away from the area as fast as possible. He has returned to his smuggling activities more assiduously than before to prepare for leaving the bakery. Mabrouk knows he can't stand much more of the Flower of Bab el-Oued and even less of his boss, though Hassan has not yet been told of his intentions. Hassan avoids referring to what happened, sensing Mabrouk's disapproval. Now the nights working in the bakery are deadly dull and also very tense. A young lad, vaguely related to Hassan, spotty and taciturn, has replaced Boualem and is slowly learning the job and how to work the kneading machine. Mabrouk does not talk to him. He hates him as much as he despises Hassan and constantly wears his earphones to show he wants to keep his distance.

Today he is pleased. His day has started well. Through a sailor he has just got hold of a batch of towels made in Hong Kong that he has to deliver to El Biar for resale. Halfway across the passageway he meets a young man wearing a leather jacket, jeans, tennis shoes, and a flowered shirt running toward the harbor with a rucksack on his back. Mabrouk stops dead. The brightly colored shirt is familiar. He puts down his bags and calls out to the young man receding in the distance, "Hey, Mess! Is that you?"

Mess stops, turns around, and smiles back at Mabrouk. Cleanshaven, not wearing his *qamis*, looking smart in new clothes, the bandy-legged emigrant is exultant.

"Hi, Mabrouk! Still at your *trabendo*?"

Mabrouk picks up his bags and hurries toward him.

"Hey! What've you done to your beard? And where the hell are you off to?"

Mess, beaming all over, takes a brown-colored passport from his pocket and waves it under Mabrouk's nose.

"Here it is! I got it in the end. Brand new! And now I'm going home."

Mabrouk snatches the passport out of Mess's hands. Mess does not stop him though he feels obliged to protest.

"Careful . . ."

"What is this?"

Mabrouk opens it and looks at the pages inside. Though he reads with difficulty, he succeeds in deciphering Mess's first and last names. He whistles in admiration.

"You're French then?"

"Yes, I bloody well am! That's what I've been trying to explain to everyone for months but no one was listening."

He swaggers, pleased to have finally been able to show someone he trusts like Mabrouk the precious document he has been admiring day and night for the last week. The association was successful in dealing with his case. Mess then went to the consulate and got his passport in a couple of hours. Since then he has been on cloud nine in a dream involving the ship; his mother, Bobigny; his tower block; and Farida, the French-Algerian girl with whom he used to smoke his first joints in the bushes behind the shopping center. Mess is convinced she will be waiting for him.

AFTER GOING OUT with her the first time, he forbade her to touch drugs. She was sixteen. He wanted her to remain pure, adolescent, naïve, a virgin . . . He liked her like that. After that first evening during which their lips touched, he started to idealize Farida. She became his mother, his sister, his wife, his daughter, his fantasy . . . He went for long walks with her around their neighborhood, spent hours kissing her in the shrubs beside the motorway, and, after a particularly good deal, would take her to a restaurant to stuff her with pizzas. He loved her silence, her vacant eyes, her madonna-like pallor.

As the months went by, Mess felt very close to her, too close, so he did not notice she was becoming more and more silent, more pale, more withdrawn. He had no idea Farida had continued to smoke joints and that things had moved on very quickly from there. Other dealers were hanging around their neighborhood like birds of prey. Farida started to use hard drugs and, to pay for her fixes, resorted inevitably to prostitution. Mess had been deported before discovering the truth and since then had been keeping the pure Farida in a corner of his heart. He had never written to her. When he spoke on the phone he never asked anyone about her. He was not like that. He knew she would be waiting for him. He was certain of it. He had no idea that Farida had been dead for months, her young life snuffed out by an overdose at the age of eighteen in the sordid toilets of the shopping center . . .

NATURALLY MESS HAD NOT told anyone of his planned departure from Algiers, and especially not his militant friends. He was sure that if, by some misfortune, Rashid were to come to hear of it, he would use his Kalashnikov to do him in. The only person he could have told was Imam Rabah. He would have understood. But the preacher had already gone back to his village. Mess was heartbroken to see him go. That was life, with its joys and sufferings. It was as simple as that . . . Now he too was leaving, crossing the sea, going to another country, his country. How wonderful!

"In twenty minutes I'll be on the ship. Ciao! I'm leaving you, Bab el-Oued, Rocher Carré, and the sunshine."

Mabrouk does not pick up the hint of gloating in Mess's words. He stammers, "You're Fren . . . you're French and you're crossing to France!"

"That's life. I'll miss you, *smina*."

He embraces Mabrouk affectionately, then walks away.

"When you get there drink a Tuborg for me!"

"Sure thing! Son of a bitch! Look after yourself!"

Mabrouk watches him disappear in the distance. Suddenly he yells, "Hey Mess! Come back! You've forgotten your passport!"

In the rush of departure, the emigrant has forgotten the precious passport. He runs back and grabs it.

"Shit! What a time to lose it!"

Mabrouk has a good laugh. He has to deliver his goods to El Biar, then intends to go and down a couple of beers at the Grande Brasserie. He won't see Boualem there. He has not seen him since he was fired. He seems to have disappeared. Mabrouk knows, as does everyone else, that there was an epic fight one night, on the rocks.

WHEN HE HAPPENED to meet Saïd the following morning, his face covered in bruises, he couldn't help smiling with satisfaction, realizing that Boualem had put up a good fight. Saïd had stopped and glared at him, threatening and contemptuous.

"Seen something funny?"

Mabrouk swallowed without answering. He had already received his share of blows and did not want any more aggravation. All at once Saïd relaxed, placed an affectionate hand on Mabrouk's shoulder, and led him down a side street.

"We're organizing a big meeting on Thursday. There's going to be a free discussion of everything. I'd really like you to come."

"Sure!"

"Guys like you, once they change and discover the word of God, they're really great. An angel passes and all is sweetness and light around them. I sense you're going to change your rough ways and calm down. You'll find happiness with us."

Mabrouk had been unable to reply to Saïd's proposals. What was the point? He had gone to the meeting. Hadn't opened his mouth. Then he started going to the mosque. It hadn't been difficult to find a *qamis* his size. He had removed his cap. But he continued with the black market. He was just like everyone else now. He was extremely cautious when going to drink his beer, and never on a Friday . . . Fat Mabrouk was beginning to discover the state of grace.

THERE IS FRANTIC ACTIVITY on the quay near the *Tassili,* the passenger ship plying between Algiers and Marseilles. Boualem is among the many passengers milling around completing the departure formalities. He doesn't notice Mess at one of the counters, in heated discussion with a suspicious policeman examining his brand-new passport. A crowd of onlookers, friends, and relations throng the railing overlooking the port, their gaze riveted to the steamer. Among them is Yamina, wearing the *hidjab,* trying to make out the figure of Boualem in the crowd of passengers walking up the gangway before disappearing into the ship.

THE FATEFUL DAY has come around very quickly. Too quickly. Since that first kiss exchanged on the terrace, time has gone by at dizzying speed. Yamina and Boualem saw one another often, spent entire afternoons together making plans for a happy future when she would finally join him.

"I'll go as far north as Norway. I've got good connections there already. Twelve mates I know. There's work on the farms. And it seems the police aren't too fussy."

"But it must be cold up there?"

"I can stand it! They say if you survive for six months the farmers can help you with your papers and the immigration services. I'll be back for you in two years' time . . ."

Yamina somehow knows he will never come back for her, yet she still feels she is already his wife. All at once she thinks she can make him out on the bridge. Her eyes fill with tears. She gives a little wave. A few yards away, Kader, also leaning on the parapet, is watching the departure, his eyes full of sadness and longing. As the ship's hooter sounds, Boualem takes the last few steps before disappearing into the ship.

At the other end of the quay Saïd is positioned near the gangway, hidden behind some large crates. He calmly brandishes his revolver and takes aim at Boualem. After the shooting he will stay where he is, waiting patiently until his militant friend from the dockers' union who let him into the port area comes to collect him and help him leave unseen.

The decision to kill Boualem took root in Saïd's mind the minute he got the revolver in his hands. He did not know why these two mysterious men had given him the weapon. One day they would no doubt give him some instructions. He knows that then he will be sucked into the spiral of violence and death. In the meantime, he hangs around Bab el-Oued, increasingly jumpy, never separated from his gun, his new companion.

He knew that Boualem frequently met his sister Yamina, that they went about together, took tea in the downtown tearooms, talked and laughed. Then he was told of Boualem's decision. "He's trying to escape abroad. He's already bought his ticket. I'm not going to let that turd get off so easily! He doesn't deserve it! Off he goes, just like that! No way!" Saïd was obsessed by this departure: he felt stymied. The fight on the rocks hadn't settled anything. He didn't really know why, but he was tormented by the way events unfolded.

He trained himself to place the bullets in the chamber of the revolver, and one night he went to a deserted beach outside the town. He used up ten bullets shooting in the air. The pleasure of the shots, the smell of the gunpowder, the feel of the weapon he was holding in his hand really turned him on. He had just discovered how exciting it was. That night he slept well, had a wonderful dream in which he was mounted on a frisky charger and galloping at the head of an army of cavalry all dressed in silk, armed with sabers. In the morning while drinking his coffee, he prepared his plan. Within two days he obtained the information he required with the help of his militant docker friend. "Yes, Boualem was leaving, but it would be a one-way trip: straight to hell!"

SAÏD IS WATCHING the gangway where Boualem has slowed down, as if hesitating. Saïd takes aim at his chest. His finger starts to squeeze the trigger. Then Boualem stops, searching in the crowd for Yamina. Saïd frowns. "Why the hell is the idiot stopping? He must really want to die!" Suddenly he lowers his weapon and sticks it in his jacket. He watches Boualem start walking again. All at once his urge to kill Boualem has completely evaporated though he cannot understand what made him change his mind. Why on earth should he prevent Boualem leaving when, if he were to follow his own secret desire, he too would be striding up the gangway to avoid this premonition of violence, blood, and death that he has? He closes his eyes, opens them once again. Now Boualem has disappeared, swallowed up in the depths of the ship. Saïd no longer cares. He looks at the city with its pall of pollution, listens to its countless sounds. A city that inspires a nameless fear in him, which he will have to face once again when the docker comes to collect him.

YAMINA AND KADER have decided to remain at the harbor until the steamer leaves. They have not noticed anything untoward on the quays. Kader half watches the sailors casting off while thinking of his Toyota.

THE WOMEN ARE SPREADING out their sheets to dry on the terrace of the block of flats. Hanifa is not as lively as usual; she is uncommunicative. From time to time she glances towards the sea hoping to catch a glimpse of the ship as it leaves the harbor. Lynda appears, a packet of books under her arm. Joyful and carefree as usual, she twirls around and shows what she has just acquired. "Hey, girls! I've got a new lot of books, steamy as hell! Love, love, nothing but love!" The young women rush toward her and grab the books, keen to read the latest adventures of their heroines. A lively discussion punctuated with laughter and jokes starts up. Hanifa doesn't listen. Lynda takes Aïcha's hand and draws her into the laundry room.

"Isn't it hot today! Aren't you fed up with your headscarf and *hidjab*? Aren't they suffocating you?"

Aïcha makes a face, still holding Lynda's hand. "Do you hate me?"

"Of course not, Aïcha! I was joking!"

Hanifa has discreetly removed herself to the far end of the terrace and hides her face as she turns toward the sea. The tears gather in her eyes as she watches, motionless, the white mass of the steamer slowly leaving, taking with it her brother Boualem. She murmurs a prayer hoping that God will bring him back safe and sound.

55

THREE YEARS HAVE PASSED. THE SUMMER IN ALGIERS IS HOT, HUMID, and dusty. The city is very tense. The bomb attacks, sabotage, various manipulations, and repression have ruined the atmosphere and are making people edgy, nervous, suspicious. No one knows what lies ahead. The pictures from Sarajevo, Kabul, Mogadishu prove that anything is possible, anything can happen, here just like everywhere else. Why Beirut, why Sarajevo, and why not Algiers?

For the past ten minutes Yamina and her mother have been riveted to the television, busy watching the third episode of a new soap on a French channel. Yamina rests her head on her mother's shoulder. She is lucky to have her. Her enthusiasm, her love of life are an invaluable support to Yamina who has been unhappy and in low spirits since Boualem left. After the soap, they switch back to a local channel to watch the news, which starts by showing a man who took part in the murder of a young police officer in Bab el-Oued. Lalla Jamila immediately turns up the volume. The man is shown back view. He looks thin. Ageless. One of his hands is shaking as he speaks, answering in a faint voice the barrage of questions put by an anonymous reporter. Apparently he is a cobbler from Bab el-Oued. Together with others he planned the murder in the forest of Bouzaréah. They set their sights on the policeman and trailed him. They were supposed to take his gun away, but he did not have it on him. When he was killed he was near his home, in his neighborhood. He was a young man who had just joined the police force, needing a job at a time of high unemployment. The young policeman was talking to his friends, leaning against the door of his block of flats. He kept on smoothing the crease of his brand-new trousers. He felt safe. He got three bullets in the head and two in the chest. After the murder, the cobbler fainted. That is all he can remember. The announcer says he was arrested by the other young men of the district. He was very nearly lynched. Is that true? They show the cobbler again. His hand continues to shake as he tries to justify himself. He was trapped. If he did not take part in the killing, his life was threatened. He had nothing against the young man, who was known and well thought of in Bab el-Oued. He himself was preparing to get married.

Lalla Jamila, looking keenly at the television pictures, bursts out, "Why don't they show us his face? Let them show us who he is; if he's a cobbler from the neighborhood, we must know him. Why don't they show us?"

Yamina jumps up suddenly, feeling she needs to throw up. Lalla Jamila, feeling depressed, turns off the set. She weeps at the thought of her son Saïd who disappeared after the Islamic demonstrations following the strike in June 1991. Is he in prison? In one of the camps in the south? In hiding? She does not know. Someone is supposed to have seen him in Oran. His younger brother, taking advantage of this unexpected good luck, is now settled in Saïd's room.

EVERY FRIDAY YAMINA GOES to the cemetery. She does not wear the *hidjab* but Lalla Jamila makes no protest, not wanting to upset her daughter who is so desperately unhappy. Yamina spends a long time at her father's grave. Sometimes she meets Hanifa in the alleys. They greet one another but can find nothing to say; they do not know how to communicate and share their unhappiness.

Hanifa is very affected by Boualem's departure; she is especially upset at having no news of him. She regularly dreams of him and has long conversations when she tells him everything that is going on in the neighborhood. But he never answers when she plies him with questions. Why doesn't he write? What country is he in? What is he doing?

Kader rarely goes to the cemetery. He has not been able to buy the Toyota of his dreams. He too has inherited his brother's bed, though this has not prevented him from having a bad year at school. He was expelled and now sells American cigarettes near the market. He is still making plans while biding his time to leave. From time to time, bursting with pleasure, he goes to the cinema with Aïcha who now wears the more severe black *jellaba* and continues her secret love games with Lynda.

Rashid died as he would have wished, a Kalashnikov in his hand, during a shoot-out with the police in the *maquis* not far from Algiers. The Peshawar period was long since gone.

Mabrouk, involved in smuggling hashish from Morocco, is now in prison serving a four-year sentence. His fellow prisoners have taught him the prayers and are instructing him in the basic tenets of Islam.

Mess went back to his Paris high-rise suburb. He works in a garage and is keeping a low profile. Sometimes when going to the workshop early in the gray mornings, he remembers the sunshine of Algiers.

Ouardya is buried in the beautiful family cemetery at Belcourt. She was found dead in her apartment a few weeks after Boualem left. The police concluded she committed suicide, using gas.

Hassan-the-baker has hired two new apprentices to work nights. He goes to the mosque regularly and avoids talking of his youth. He let his beard grow when the Islamists were growing more powerful, then shaved it off when the situation became more complex. Seeing the escalation of violence, he is seriously thinking of withdrawing to his village in Kabylia.

When they got back to France, Paulo Gasen and his aunt showed their photos of Algiers and recounted their experiences; Mme Gasen has not given up hope of returning one day. Paulo is planning to set up a joint Franco-Algerian company the minute they stop killing foreigners over there.

The women continue to meet on the terrace where the loudspeaker is no longer in use now since new laws forbid the broadcasting of sermons. They are as passionately interested as ever in the Harlequin collection, though it is more difficult for books to get through these days.

Imam Rabah was living peacefully in his village in the Aurès mountains until an armed group of Islamists decided to seek refuge in his small mosque. He could not refuse them hospitality. One night the mosque was surrounded by the army. A few shells reduced it to ruins, together with its occupants. Imam Rabah died at prayer.

Aami Mourad chose to die of systemic cancer, which he refused to have treated, feeling the time had come for him to bow out.

Ammar the postman still has not been able to afford the perfume glamorous Lamia demanded in exchange for her possible favors. He has been worried for some time now about staff cutbacks. With his five children to feed, he cannot bear thinking about losing his job.

About the Book

Bored housewives, kept in seclusion, pulling the latest Harlequin romances up on a string through the stairwell. Young men transformed from drunken thugs in jeans and T-shirts into Islamic militants in beards and flowing white robes. A baker unwittingly caught in a web of intrigue, an imam whose faith is tested by urban corruption, a lonely divorcée accused of prostitution—all take part in Merzak Allouache's compelling novel of a society on the brink of crisis.

Allouache tells the story of the people of Bab el-Oued, a poor neighborhood in contemporary Algiers. His experience as a filmmaker lends the work a cinematic quality, bringing it vibrantly and immediately to life. *Bab el-Oued*'s memorable characters draw us into their world. Entering their lives, we come to appreciate the human costs of economic and political decline and also to understand something of the reasons underlying the power of new and violent forms of Islamic militancy.

"I wrote this book," said Algerian director **Merzak Allouache**, "to exorcise the many frustrations that arose when making the film *Bab el-Oued City* in Algiers. Writing the book gave me a sense of freedom not possible with the constraints of the camera, especially when shooting in a hostile environment, as was the case there." *Bab el-Oued City*, released to wide acclaim in 1993, is Allouache's fifth full-length film. He now lives in France.

Angela Brewer, a professional linguist and literary translator, spent her early years in the Middle East, where she has traveled widely. She now lives in Western Europe.